The Cave

2/19/14

The Cave Where The Water Always Drips

by Robert DeMayo

Robert DeMayo

First Printing July 2009
Wayward Publishing (1989)

Copies of this book can be ordered at:
www.lulu.com/waywardtravelers
and   amazon.com

Or found locally in the Sedona, AZ area.

Edited by: **Nina Rehfeld**
Nina@txture.com

Cover model: **Gina Reeder**

Cover design & photo by: **Robert DeMayo**

Water Cave symbol created by: **Lovejoy**
lovejoy@lovejoycreations.com

This story is a work of fiction.
All characters and events are creations
of the author.

There are many tales of lost treasure from the Sedona area, and although Montezuma's treasure may not be on the top of the list, the Lost Coconino Gold Mine was around here somewhere (it still hasn't been found); and it was supposedly located in a box canyon with a hidden entrance. There have also been quite a few pieces of Spanish armor found in nearby Sycamore Canyon—so we know they were here.

The Yavapai/Apache do have a creation myth for this area, and it is told here through the voice of a character named Saan, but any explanation of the myth in this publication is the work of the author.

Sincerely yours,

Robert DeMayo
65 View Dr.
Sedona, AZ 86336
Rdemayo07@aol.com

Robert DeMayo

"We love the quiet; we suffer the mouse to play; when the woods are rustled by the wind, we fear not."
(Indian Chief to the Penn. governor, 1796)

"Be scared. You can't help that. But don't be afraid. Ain't nothing in the woods going to hurt you unless you corner it, or it smells that you are afraid."
(William Faulkner)

"What is life? It is the flash of a firefly in the night... it is the little shadow which runs across the grass and loses itself in the Sunset.
(Crowfoot, Blackfoot Confederacy, 1890)

"A man's life is interesting primarily when he has failed...for it's a sign he tried to surpass himself."
(Georges Clemenceau)

"But let judgment run down as waters, and righteousness as a mighty stream."
(The Bible, Amos 5:24)

"The sword conquered for a while, but the spirit conquers forever!"
(Sholem Asch)

Robert DeMayo

The Cave Where The Water Always Drips

for Diana

Robert DeMayo

Chapter One

He strode into the lecture hall wearing an almost manic look of pride. Black hair, a neatly-trimmed goatee, Hispanic features—Marcos DeNiza looked well at thirty.

His eyes were full of confidence, but it came from something other than his good looks.

He had a secret.

The hall was crowded, and not many noticed his arrival; which irritated him a little, but not enough to dampen his mood.

He cleared his throat and turned on a projector.

"Attention everyone, can I have your attention?"

Impatiently, he switched off the lights.

"I want to thank you all for coming, but I have an early day tomorrow so let's get started."

Half the crowd was still standing; they quickly found seats, unhappy in being rushed.

He hit the first slide; a projection of a Conquistador's helmet.

Smiling broadly, he pointed at it.

"Your pioneers were not the first ones to explore this area; it was the Spanish," said Marcos. "They had a presence in Arizona for hundreds of years."

The next slide was an old map of the Southwest.

"New Spain was south of us. They called this area *Tierra Incognita* — an unknown land."

He smiled showing perfect teeth.

The next few slides showed a series of Spanish explorers. Marcos recited the names as each new slide appeared: "Tovar," (slide) "Gardenas," (slide) "Onate," (slide) "Espejo — the list goes on. They risked their lives to come to a land of brutal Indians and unforgiving terrain."

He then asked, "Can anyone tell me why they were so tenacious?"

Marcos beamed with pride. Nobody dared interrupt him.

He flipped a large gold coin into the air and smiled as he caught it. Everyone in the room stared at the coin, mesmerized.

"Gold!" said Marcos.

"Not just a small amount of gold, mind you," he added. "This was a place of riches."

He inhaled slowly as he scanned the room.

"It was a place with treasures that could drive weak men insane."

The next few slides were of old mines, ruins and drawings. He continued with his narration.

"The seven cities of Cibola; where the streets were lined with gold," (slide) "the lost Coconino gold mine," (slide) "the lost Dutchman's mine." (slide)

"These are just a few, but if you live in Arizona, you are familiar with tales of lost treasure."

The next slide was of two Spanish explorers. It was a powerful shot, their faces full of emotion. They bore a strong resemblance to Marcos.

"It was no different back then," declared Marcos.

He hit the next slide; an image of a mound of Aztec gold came up, complete with gold masks, gold plates, and countless gold chains.

Marcos made a dramatic gesture, "Many of them were looking for this, Montezuma's gold."

A few in the crowd laughed.

He rubbed the back of his neck vigorously.

"You dare laugh at me? It exists!" He stared at the crowd looking for a challenger.

Angered, he continued, "You have my word. I believe..."

A young woman in her early twenties arrived late and screeched a chair as she moved to a seat. Her name was Jules Collins, and she wore her black hair tied back over a button-up collared shirt, and carried a camera.

Marcos was looking offended, and said, "I hope I haven't kept you from anything, Miss."

"No. Sorry. Did I interrupt you?" she asked, putting on her best smile.

"My family has been waiting hundreds of years for this moment, what will a few more minutes matter?" said Marcos.

"I said I was sorry," she said again. "I write for the College paper and was sent to take your picture. I just heard about your expedition."

She held up her camera like it was a press pass.

Marcos smiled broadly.

"I see. You are here to document my announcement of an imminent discovery?"

Jules laughed, and quickly tried to quell it, but didn't do a great job.

Marcos couldn't believe her rudeness.

"Excuse me?" he said.

Jules knew she was in trouble, but couldn't hold her tongue. "You can announce an expedition; but you can't announce a discovery before you do it."

Marcos lost his cool completely.

"I can," he screamed. "I can say whatever I want, because I will find it."

He grabbed the desk firmly, puffed up his chest, and stated, "It is my destiny!"

The crowd was quiet as they took in the show.

Jules was fighting not to laugh.

"Okay. Again, I'm sorry," she pleaded.

He looked past her and addressed the room, saying proudly, "Tomorrow I depart to find this treasure."

The crowd erupted into nervous laughter.

He ignored them, "Seriously, I have gathered you here today to announce it."

Jules raised her camera. "How can you be so certain?" she asked.

Marcos fingered the remote, and they were shown an image of a map. It was strange map; like a stick-figured centipede with a circular symbol on the top center.

"Because I have a map," said Marcos. "And this map is one of a kind. It will tell me where the treasure is."

He flipped his gold coin in the air again.

Jules stared at the map, which was really just a bunch of thick black lines linked together. And then her attention was riveted to the circular symbol on the top of the map.

She remained seated, but all the color had left her face. She raised a slightly shaking hand.

"What is that symbol on the top?" she asked.

Marcos spoke patiently, and offered his explanation slowly. "This is a symbol my ancestor used to designate where the treasure was."

Jules stared at it for a minute before replying, "I've seen it before."

Marcos was condescending in his reply. "I would find that highly unlikely."

While Marcos continued to explain his upcoming expedition, Jules remembered a trip with her father, ten years ago.

She thought of her father's old station wagon as they turned off the Interstate onto a dirt road. A partially shot-gunned sign read: Indian Reservation.

Her father, George, was in his early forties, and had just found religion. It had not seemed a bad thing when it had pulled him out of depression, but then he'd started changing. Not long ago he had started dressing like some kind of missionary, and he never went anywhere without a bible.

He looked nervous, and a bit revolted, as he surveyed the reservation. He constantly fingered a cross hanging from his neck as he talked.

"This was a bad idea. We shouldn't have come," said George. "If we leave now we'll have a good start on Montana."

Jules looked at her father, and said, "You promised mom you'd bring me here."

George was silent for a minute before he replied. "Your mother is no longer with us. I think we should at the very least move on in the morning."

On the side of the road was an old woman. She looked ancient as she chanted and shook a stick at George's car. Her name was Saan.

"This one here's your kin," said George. "Each year she looks more like an old raven."

Saan waved again, determined to make him pull over for her; he stopped the station wagon.

As the old woman approached the car George turned to Jules.

"I told your mother I'd do this," he said. "But now I don't know; I wish I had guidance."

He glanced at the rear view mirror.

Jules pleaded with her father, "Dad, they're family, and you promised."

He corrected her, "Their blood may flow through your veins, but not mine." He met her eyes, and added, "And I made that promise to your mother before I'd experienced salvation; before I'd found Jesus, or ..."

Saan interrupted them by banging on the window and George almost jumped out of his skin.

Later, Jules and George sat with a group around a fire. There were about twenty people; everyone seemed to know each other—and Jules.

As the sky darkened someone threw several logs on the fire. Sparks danced all around. The heavens were full of stars.

Saan stepped out of the shadows, now dressed in ceremonial clothes. She shook a rattle as she walked.

"Before First Woman was born our ancestors come up from the underworld," said Saan.

She smiled at Jules' father as she walked around the fire. She seemed youthful as she chanted. Her step was light.

The fire roared to life.

Saan continued, "They come up and they lived in the sun. They were happy, they were."

Again she circled the fire, but when she reappeared the smile had left her face. She had mysteriously aged and now seemed angry.

"Then, there was a big flood," said Saan, "and many died. Many. Many."

She stared at everyone, and was very serious as she said, "Do something wrong and the rains come."

Jules' father looked away nervously; Saan stared at him for a silent moment before she continued, but now her tone was light again, as if there was hope.

"But First Woman lived, she did," continued Saan. "She was the only one that lived 'cause she floated up in a hollow log."

The old woman stopped and looked at Jules. "They sealed her up in it, they did."

Jules fidgeted in her stare.

"Don't worry, she wasn't alone," said Saan. "No. A bird helped her. And she also had with her a precious White Stone."

Saan looked around again, seriously. "Got that stone from the underground world, she did."

Jules' father got up and walked away. He walked quickly, but he could still hear her words.

"And she had a good hidin' spot," said Saan. "Now that's something everyone needs; a place where you can rest."

Saan smiled and circled the fire again, chanting as she went. On the back of her dress was a large, circular design or symbol.

As Jules returned from her daydream, she saw the same symbol, which was now highlighted by a pointer in Marcos´ hand.

The symbol appeared to be of a cave, with water puddled on the floor. There was a red handprint on the ceiling, and something gold near the back wall.

Marcos pointed at it again, and said, "This is where I will find my treasure — in this cave."

Jules hesitated, but then spoke her mind, "You call it *your* treasure?"

Marcos looked around the room nervously.

"It *is* my treasure," he stammered. "It belongs to my family. We have known of it for over 300 years."

Jules knew her question would infuriate him, but she asked anyway, "But what about the symbol? It doesn't look Spanish to me."

Marcos fought for self control, and then spoke in a voice heavy with mock patience, "Oh, are we back to that again?"

Jules stared at the floor, and quietly replied, "Well, it just seems odd."

He held up the gold coin again, and tried his best to be charming.

"This is not just a piece of gold. This is an Aztec coin. It was found nearby, not in Mexico."

He stared at Jules, and then everyone else.

Then he added defiantly, "I found it!"

Jules was angry, but she flashed him a disarming smile. She then took out a pad and pen, and said, "Forgive me; I'm just trying to get everything straight for my article."

He nodded, straightened his shirt, and stood tall.

"I am an established archaeologist, not some amateur treasure hunter," said Marcos.

He stared at Jules, "And surely you don't expect me to give away all the details on the night before my expedition?"

He returned to the slide of the two conquistadors.

"I have dedicated my life to finding this treasure," said Marcos. "Only a recent discovery made all this possible."

All became silent as he held up the gold coin.

He started to speak reverently, "Three hundred years ago two of my ancestors searched for this treasure. They found something, but nobody believed them."

Marcos seemed to lose himself as he stared at the gold coin, and continued, almost to himself.

"For generations we have been ridiculed."

He walked to the wall and flipped on the lights.

"Tomorrow I set out to restore my family's honor by rediscovering the treasure."

He stepped back to applause.

The two conquistadors continued to stare from the screen.

Chapter Two

ARIZONA TERRITORY 1705

The desert brush of prickly-pear cactus and scrub oak gave way to limestone cliffs of red and yellow. They rose thousands of feet up to form the Colorado plateau, their upper slopes covered with Ponderosa Pines.

Ahead, one large canyon penetrated straight in.

Two Spanish explorers approached the canyon on mules loaded with gear. They each wore helmets and breast plates, and were well armed with muzzle-loaders and pistols.

They were Fernando DeNiza, a tall, bearded man in his late twenties, and his younger brother, Antonio. Fernando took the lead with a determined stare.

Antonio smiled as he took off his helmet and looked around. His face was youthful, and untried.

Fernando threatened to backhand him, and ordered, "Keep it on, little brother; there are things worse than a sore head."

Antonio pleaded with him.

"Come on Fernando. We've been riding since the port of Guaymas—I feel like I've spent a year in this saddle."

"You exaggerate; it has only been two months. And we have traveled far, because what we search for is great. It is hidden in one of these canyons, so keep your eyes open," warned Fernando.

Antonio laughed, "You are too serious, hermano; you should relax."

"I will not!" replied Fernando. "And you should not either. Your casual attitude will someday cost you your life."

Then he added with a laugh, "With my luck it will cost my life as well."

Fernando took out his pistol and checked it.

He said, "What we search for is well protected, of that I have been warned."

He stared at several Indian scalps dangling on the side of his saddle.

Antonio looked real nervous, "What do you mean protected?"

Fernando hesitated, and then said, "They say a witch guards the treasure."

Antonio immediately crossed himself, and muttered, "Sangre de Cristo, what next?"

Fernando laughed, "We are modern men, and we do not fear witches. Besides, this is a stroke of luck."

His brother stared at him, confused.

Fernando continued, "The witch lives by the treasure, and the local Indians consider the place to be taboo."

"How is that good for us?" asked Antonio.

"Because once we get the treasure they will not attack. The witch's canyon will be our sanctuary."

Antonio rubbed the back of his neck, and said, "Could've mentioned all that earlier."

Fernando stared him down, "If you had learned some Indian like I told you, you would have heard."

Antonio looked terrified. "Do you think knowing Indian will make me safer?"

Fernando looked at the scalps. "It didn't help them."

He scanned the cliffs they were approaching, and said, "Just keep your helmet on."

Above them, on the cliff top, sat an old Indian. He was out of sight on the canyon rim, and watched the two Spaniards moving through the canyon below.

He was Nantan Lupan, or Grey Wolf, and his white hair and wise eyes hinted that he was named well. While watching he barely moved.

A younger warrior, Bidzill, or He is Strong, approached and angrily pointed at the two men in the canyon.

"We should kill them now," said Bidzill.

Grey Wolf smiled at the young man, and cautioned him, "We do not rush into things. If they only pass through I will allow it."

Bidzill was shocked and fired back, "You belong by the fire with the women. A warrior..."

Grey Wolf held up his hand, silencing Bidzill.

"You will obey me," said Grey Wolf. "When we rush into things only death comes of it. I have spoken."

After a moment he asked, "Have you seen my grandson Aditsan?"

Bidzill was frustrated, and replied sarcastically. "He is probably picking flowers."

Grey Wolf shook his head. "Picking flowers is not so bad."

Bidzill stormed off. It was obvious he was not happy.

* * *

As everyone else left the lecture hall, Jules took a few pictures of Marcos and checked the spelling of his name.

"I didn't mean to put you on the spot back there," she said, apologetically.

He began to snap at her, but faltered as she took off her glasses and smiled at him.

"I must have been mistaken about the symbol," she said. "You certainly seem to know what you're doing."

He was smitten and now he talked freely.

"All my ancestors knew was the treasure was in the Arizona Territory. They had a map of a canyon, but there are many canyons here."

Jules looked at the gold coin.

"And when you found that coin," she said. "You knew where to use the map."

Marcos smiled broadly. "Precisely."

For a moment he stared at Jules, hesitating, and finally pulled out a transparent sheet with the lines from the map drawn out.

He then laid out a topographical map and pointed to a canyon.

Jules noted the canyon mentally.

"This is where I found the coin," said Marcos.

He took the transparent sheet and laid it over the topographical map.

"You see how it lines up?" said Marcos.

Jules couldn't believe it. They matched perfectly. What had before looked like a crazy collection of lines suddenly made sense when aligned with a modern map.

Jules asked, "Who made this map?"

Marcos stared into the distance, and momentarily stopped his narration. He had a far-away stare on his pale face.

As she watched him, he shuddered, while some terrible image seemed to flash through his mind.

Jules grew impatient, and asked, "Professor, did the maker of this map find something?"

Marcos stared at his map, and then without meeting her eyes, he looked at his shoes, and said,

Robert DeMayo

"Yes, he most definitely did."

*   *   *

Fernando walked through a narrow canyon, a shallow creek cutting through its floor. The high walls rose up into the sunlight, far above.

Small trout darted out of his way as he waded through the shallow water.

As he walked his mule up the stream the splashes of his footsteps echoed.

Around the bend, just ahead, something splashed.

"Show yourself!" he shouted

He turned the bend, but there was nothing in sight to explain the noise. As he stood listening he could hear footsteps echoing again, and then distant singing.

He yelled, "Coward!"

In the water by his feet something golden sparkled. He bent down to pick it up.

With his ear by the water he heard a soft whispering. And then the dark sandstone walls suddenly wailed, as if they could feel pain, and voice it.

A hard rain started out of nowhere, soaking the red walls and giving them a deep blood color.

The water drained into the narrow canyon and immediately, the creek started to rise

Chapter Three

Marcos drove a 4x4 Jeep up a twisting highway. The top was down and he marveled at the beauty of the place. The summer heat was oppressive, but as he went deeper into the canyon it got cooler.

Through the tops of the ponderosa pines he saw limestone cliffs, yellowing as they rose.

To his right a creek flowed through the canyon, its banks lined with ancient sycamore trees. Tourists were parked along the road taking photos, and inevitably causing traffic chaos.

Marcos cursed them; again and again, as he had to sharply slow down.

He turned on the radio, *"...who knows when the drought will break, but we could sure use those monsoon rains. With only scattered showers..."*

Once deep into the canyon, he pulled over to the left and parked near a sign that read: West Fork Trailhead.

Marcos reached into the back seat and took out a large backpack. He shouldered it, and started collecting a heap of other gear.

A few yards away, Jules had sunk down low into her driver's seat, spying on Marcos. The bored look on her face disappeared when he pulled up, and for a second, she stopped chewing on the apple that she had been munching away at.

Her window was open only a crack.

Just before departing, Marcos looked at his jeep, which was still open with the top down. He glanced at the sky, put his hand on the canopy, then decided it was a waste of time to put it up, and turned to go.

Both Jules and Marcos noticed some boys tossing rocks at an old raven sitting on a low fence. The raven seemed ancient, but still managed to dodge the rocks.

When Jules looked back Marcos had started down the trail. Just as he was about to enter a narrow canyon, a ranger approached him and blocked his way. Marcos was so lost in thought that he actually tried to walk around him.

"I hope you're not planning on hiking in that far," said the ranger.

Marcos was baffled that someone would try to stop him at all. "What could you possibly mean?"

The ranger rubbed his chin. "Well, this time of year even a little rain will bring on a flash flood. That canyon is a death trap."

Marcos set down his pack and said, "I hadn't realized." He paused for a minute, and then added, "But it doesn't look like rain today; I'll keep my eyes open."

The ranger shook his head, "You don't understand. I can't possibly let you go in there."

Marcos rubbed the back of his neck. "It takes more than a little weather to stop me."

The ranger stood a bit taller. "Then we have a problem because Arizona doesn't like paying for senseless rescues. Can't you just go somewhere else?"

Marcos flushed red. "No."

Then he warned, "And I know important people who could force you allow me."

The ranger laughed, "Look, I'm just trying to keep you from getting killed. There's logic behind what I'm saying. Go do something other than hiking a flash flood zone at the start of the monsoon season."

Marcos scratched his ear, and then resigned, "You're right, I'll find another trail."

He shrugged his shoulders. "I was foolish to be so persistent."

The ranger wished him luck and walked off. When he was out of sight Marcos shouldered his pack and quickly headed down the trail.

Once he was out of sight Jules opened her door and stepped out, looking fit and determined. She wore hiking boots, shorts and a red bandana.

She shouldered a backpack which was smaller than the one Marcos was carrying, but had a sleeping bag and a small tarp attached to the outside. Before she locked the door, she glanced at the sky, and then reached around and rolled the window up tight.

The boys were still teasing the raven.

Jules threw her apple core at one of them, hitting him in the back.

"Ouch!" he yelled. "What's up with that?"

Jules ordered, "Leave 'im alone."

The kid shrugged. "It's just a bird."

Jules picked up a rock and stared at him, "You want another one?"

He stepped away. "Crazy bitch."

She raised the rock a little higher and he trudged off with his buddies.

Jules stared at the old raven.

From her shirt pocket she produced an aged photo of herself with her mother and another woman. Jules looked around six; her mother was wearing a Native American buckskin dress that was decorated with beads. Everyone was smiling.

The third person in the image was Saan. Even though she was younger, you could still make out a seriousness behind her smile.

There was actually a large raven perched on Saan's shoulder. Its beak was near her ear, as if telling secrets.

She stared at the photo for a moment, and then carefully put it away. As she followed in Marcos's footsteps, she remembered more of her last visit to the reservation.

Jules sat next to Saan after the ceremony was over. The others had left, and the fire was down to coals. Saan put her hand on the young girl's knee.

"You can call me Auntie," she said. "It's been a while since we met, but I knew you when you were little."

Then she added, "And of course I knew your mother well."

Jules stared at the coals for a minute before replying, "I can't believe she's gone, she was so full of life."

Saan nodded and smiled, "I remember her."

She seemed to drift off, then added, "When she was a young girl she used to run through the woods like a deer. She had an old spirit, that one. We all grieved when she left us, we did."

Jules couldn't seem to find her words, and then she spit it all out at once. "Before she died, she made my father promise to bring me back," she cried.

"He said he would, but since her death he's found religion and now it all seems so complicated. He wants us to leave in the morning."

Saan seemed incredulous "But we are your people. You come from here, and I've been looking forward to your visit for some time now."

Jules agreed, "I have too. My mother loved you all so much, and she wanted me to come back."

The old woman seemed to take this all rather hard. It took her a minute to compose herself.

She finally said, "My child, you are all we have left of her."

Jules dried her eyes, and stared at Saan, "How do you know these stories are true, Auntie?"

Saan laughed. "Oh, they're true all right. You wouldn't question them if you'd been raised here, like your mother."

Jules nodded. "My dad's found Jesus. Do you believe in Jesus?"

She laughed again, it was almost a cackle. "I wish I could tell you it was all the same—Great Spirit or Jesus—but the truth is, I don't know about the white people. I don't know who they are, or where they come from."

The old woman shuffled around looking for another piece of wood. Jules watched the symbol on her back. After a minute Saan continued, "All I know is there is a secret canyon near here and that's where your people come from."

Jules pleaded with her, "But how could it be so? How can people be created from sun and water?"

Saan smiled, and said, "It was not just sun and water, child. After First Woman floated to safety in the log she was very lonely, so she climbed up the mountain to see the sun."

The old woman couldn't resist shaking her rattle for effect.

"But it frightened her so she ran to the Cave Where the Water Always Drips and hid there." She hesitated as she stirred the coals in the fire, and then added, "When the water hit her, that's when she got pregnant."

Jules was confused, "But it doesn't make sense."

This amused Saan as well," It doesn't have to child. Life is messy. But it happened."

Jules insisted, "But you said you know where this area is. Has anyone ever found the cave?"

Saan gave her a sly look, "Some may know, but they are quiet. It is sacred to us. For most the cave remains hidden."

"But if the story is true, why hasn't anyone ever found the Cave Where the Water Always Drips?" asked Jules.

Saan shrugged her shoulders, "Maybe it was never meant to be found. Where there is light, there is darkness. Could be the elders had a reason to keep it hidden." Then she laughed, "It must've been a good hiding spot if nobody ever found it."

Then Saan looked at Jules for a long time before speaking. Finally she took a deep breath, and said, "What I am about to tell you I have been sworn never to repeat."

The serious look on her face scared Jules, and she asked, "Are you sure you should be telling me?"

Saan nodded, said, "Yes, I am."

"Once, when your mother was young she disappeared for several days," Saan began her story. "We weren't worried, because she was a child of the forest and from time to time she wandered, she did."

"But when she returned that time she was different. She seemed to have grown wiser, and she didn't waste words — seems to me that she had become a woman out there."

Jules was anxious to find out why. "What happened? Where had she been?"

Saan smiled, and said, "Your mother claimed she found a hidden box canyon, and in the back of it was a cave where water always dripped. She said she had stayed there overnight."

"Did she tell you where it was?" asked Jules.

Saan shook her head. "No, she wouldn't. She made me swear I would never tell another soul. In all these years you are the only one I've told."

"Do you think it was *the* cave?" asked Jules.

"Who could say," stated Saan sadly.

The young girl looked defeated, "So in other words it's lost again. Nobody knows where it is except my mother, and she's gone. And now my dad is going to take me away."

Jules sighed, "Tell me one thing that is real."

Saan's expression turned serious again, "I will tell you the name of the girl that lived in the cave."

The old woman leaned forward and whispered something into Jules´s ear. Jules heard the word and repeated it to herself.

* * *

The walls of the canyon were growing closer, their steep slopes now covered with towering pines in place of stunted pinions.

The brothers followed a creek up the canyon. They looked solemn as they scanned the cliff tops.

Fernando noticed that his younger brother was hesitant. "Not so anxious to take off your helmet now, eh?" he teased.

Antonio looked scared. "We are not alone."

Fernando nodded in response; they continued in silence.

Later, Fernando lead his mule upstream, and then stopped at a fork in the creek. The main stream continued upward, a smaller tributary flowed in from the left, coming out of an even narrower, high-walled canyon.

Fernando looked over the scene, and then made a quick decision. He said, "We separate here."

He began to divide their gear, saying, "I will explore the west fork, you continue on the main creek until you summit on the plateau."

Antonio turned pale and began to protest, but his older brother cut him off.

"Obey me, Antonio. Go to the top of the canyon, and then return to this point. You will be fine."

Antonio shook his head, "I don't like this place. "

Fernando laughed at his fear.

This was too much for Antonio, "Don't laugh at me. I hear things."

"It is all in your mind," said Fernando.

Antonio protested, "No. I hear singing."

"I think it's been too long since you bedded a woman," said Fernando.

"Don't play with me, brother. I know you feel something too," cried Antonio.

Fernando stared at his brother, hard, without uttering a word. Finally, he said, "What you sense is my treasure, and I will not leave without it."

Antonio seemed on the verge of panic. Fernando reassured him, "You'll be fine. If you have troubles go down to the open desert where the Indians cannot sneak up on you. They're brave fighters, but they respect the damage a gun can do."

Antonio shook his head again, "I will not abandon you."

Fernando suddenly became enraged, and screamed at his brother, "I'm not leaving without the treasure!" He slapped Antonio's mule and it moved upstream.

He shouted after him, "You will wait for me here, by this fork, unless you have trouble."

Antonio nodded. As he rode away, he heard his brother yell, "Keep your powder dry and your breastplate on."

Reluctantly, Antonio continued up the main canyon. His face was etched with fear as he scanned the cliff tops.

Unseen, Bidzill watched the two Spaniards unpack by the river's fork. A young warrior approached him and sat. He was Aditsan, or Listener; barely twenty, he had a dreamy look in his eyes as he stared at Bidzill.

Bidzill could see that Aditsan was in a good mood, so he purposefully ignored him.

Aditsan looked around to make sure nobody else could hear him, and then leaned over to Bidzill, and said, "I saw a girl today, across the creek by the narrow canyon."

Aditsan remembered leaning over the creek to get a drink; when he'd lifted his head he could see her. She had moved like a nervous doe, staying in the shadows.

She was beautiful.

She had spotted him quickly and they held each other's gaze for what seemed a long time. Then she'd smiled and quickly disappeared into the bushes.

Bidzill swelled with authority, and asked, "What were you doing there? That canyon is taboo."

Aditsan shook his head, and said, "No, only the canyon where the witch lives, and I saw no witch — only a beautiful girl. She smiled at me."

Bidzill was irritated by his happiness. As Grey Wolf approached he motioned Aditsan to be silent. He looked back into the canyon and saw the men separate.

Bidzill called Grey Wolf's attention, "Do you see? There. The mean one has turned off. He cannot leave that way."

Grey Wolf exhaled, and said, "You are correct. He is yours."

Bidzill expanded in his eagerness, but Grey Wolf warned him. "Take precautions. He heads into the land of the witch. If you see her you will die soon."

Bidzill was infuriated. "I am not afraid of witches."

Grey Wolf held up his hand for silence. "Hear my words now, if you take one breath of air in the witch's canyon you will die."

Bidzill stood defiantly, "I am to fear a hidden canyon? I will kill her as well if I see her."

Grey Wolf shook his head sadly. He looked down into the canyon far below and sighed. "You would be better off leaving an offering."

Bidzill walked away, angrily.

Grey Wolf called after him, "Do not touch the other stranger unless he leaves the main canyon."

Chapter Four

Marcos set off at a fast pace, following the creek that flowed down the narrow canyon floor. Before long he was sweating from carrying the large pack.

He kept up a pretty good pace until he was about a mile in. Then he started to survey the canyon walls a bit more carefully.

As he passed a small wash on his right he pulled out his map. Taking a marker, he darkened the bottom right line on the map.

He did this throughout the morning. He stopped at a dry wash, found it on his map, and darkened the spot.

The path he took had him splashing through the creek in his new boots. Every now and then he stopped, and for a second he still heard splashing.

He shouted, "Hello," and it echoed through the canyon. He smiled, "Echoes."

But then, just as he was about to continue, he heard other footsteps sounding off the high walls.

He froze, and sank down. Marcos was all bravado, and little courage. As the pursuer got closer he turned pale and sat, sweating profusely.

Then the other footsteps stopped. Marcos continued, slowly and constantly looking behind him. The situation began to anger him, and he finally summed up the courage to wait and face his follower.

Just as the pursuer came around a big rock Marcos screamed and attacked.

Jules jumped back, lifting her legs in mid-air and kicking him in the ribs. He gasped and moved again to grab her, filled with an adrenaline rush. From her stance it was obvious she'd had some form of martial art training.

Marcos was red with rage as he screamed, "How dare you follow me?"

Jules put her hand forward, as a warning, and said, "Keep your hands off me."

He took a step toward her, but she grabbed a rock and raised it in defense.

"You better stop," she said.

He felt like a caged animal. His eyes seemed to dance around in his head as he contemplated how this would affect his plans.

"I should have known you were after my treasure. I should have seen it," Marcos hissed.

Jules pointed her finger at him, and said, "I don't care about your stupid treasure.

It was obvious Marcos didn't believe her. Sarcastically, he asked, "Then please, tell me why you are here?"

Jules dropped the rock. "It's none of your business."

Marcos couldn't believe she simply evaded his question. Or that she could have the unmitigated gall to just follow him.

He said, "I could have you arrested."

She laughed, but he added, "I could have you thrown in jail."

Jules stopped. "Like it or not Marcos, this is a free country and this is a public trail—I can hike here." He rubbed his neck and then spoke.

"If you come with me, you give up all rights to the treasure," said Marcos. "Even to be named in the discovery of it."

Jules put on her most polite smile, and said, "Fine."

But that was not enough for Marcos. "And you will assist me, both as a documentarian, and in setting up a camp."

Jules just wanted the whole scene over, so she agreed, "Okay. Whatever. Let's get moving."

They continued up the trail together.

Throughout the day Marcos constantly checked his map against incoming washes. Jules couldn't keep her eyes off it.

He noticed, and taunted her. "For someone who does not believe in my treasure," said Marcos, "you seem to have a great interest in my map."

Jules laughed, "It's not that I don't believe in your treasure, I am just not interested in it."

Marcos shook his head, "You really think I'll buy that?"

She tried to change the subject. "I just don't understand what you are doing!"

He impatiently stopped, pointed to one of the washes, and said, "This wash is dry, but when it rains it would be a small river."

She looked at it. "Okay, so what?"

He held up his map and pointed. "When my map was made it was raining and all of these washes were flowing." He indicated the map. "See, they are all shown clearly."

Jules looked around and said, "I don't know if you'd want to be here then."

She pointed at the map, and added, "I've never seen a map like that. Where did you get it?"

Marcos quickly rolled it up.

He said, "This is just a photocopy. The original is far too delicate to treat like this."

Jules leaned forward. "Will you let me see it?"

Marcos moved to reply, then decided not to and walked off without speaking. He wore a grave look on his face.

Jules laughed, and ran after him. "Come on Marcos, let me see it."

He straightened his back and marched away. "I don't think so."

But she teased, "Why not? Come on, Marcos. Please? It's your map isn't it? Do you have to ask permission from someone?"

He looked shocked. "It is my map; I can do with it what I please."

Later, in the tent, Marcos took the end off a plastic cylinder and slid out a rolled up bundle. He unwrapped it, and slowly revealed an aged piece of leather.

On it was the same tangle of lines, but they were dark red and cracked. Jules leaned forward and examined them.

As Jules looked closer, her expression turned to disgust, "These lines seem like they were made from..."

"...blood," Marcos finished her sentence. "That's right. The symbol on the top was painted, but the lines came from the blood of my ancestors. They came from his wounds."

Jules was confused, and asked, wide-eyed. "But how can that be?"

Marcos took a breath, and then began: "Fernando was running from something, of that I'm sure. But he was also leaving something. Something he planned to return for. Something he could not live without. So he needed a map to get back to the place he was escaping from."

Jules paled a little. "And?" she asked softly.

"Well he didn't have a pen, or a GPS, so he used what he had on him."

* * *

Fernando uneasily backed down the narrow canyon; the sky overhead was dark and forbidding. Great bolts of lightning flashed from all directions. The rain came down with Biblical fury. From the cliffs all around it funneled down and flowed into the narrow canyon. Anything in its path was washed away.

Fernando saw that he would drown if he stayed his course. He had to make a quick getaway. He looked scared as he started to run. But then the Spaniard stopped and looked back where he had come from.

His eyes wild with panic, he took out a large knife and unbuttoned his shirt.

Teeth clenched, he touched the knife to his chest and drew it down; his scream was lost in the building wind. He turned and ran; his blood flowed with the rain.

A short way down the canyon he passed another tributary to his side and carved another gash into his chest.

Lightning took out a tree near him and he hurried to the next tributary and made his mark again.

Over and over, he cut into his flesh, making a map of his chest.

He continued in agony, the blood from his wound coloring the rising water red.

*   *   *

In the middle of the night, Marcos sat up and started screaming. His eyes were wide as Jules tried to calm him down. He finally relaxed a bit, and tried to compose himself.

"I am sorry," he said. "I have always been troubled by nightmares. They will not let me be."

Jules looked at him squarely. "Is it always the same dream?"

He nodded.

"In my dream I am always running," he began. "And I am terrified as I stumble, exhausted. I am bleeding from numerous cuts, and there is a nasty gouge above one of my eyes."

His gaze was filled with fear.

Jules handed him some water. "It sounds like something that happened to Fernando."

Marcos nodded. "But that is not the worst part. In the dream I look behind me and see a wall of water emerge, rising up as the canyon narrows, as if to grab me."

He stared at her. "As it crashes I wake up."

Jules picked up the map with all the lines traced on it and shook her head, "It's no wonder you have nightmares with a map made from your ancestor´s blood. Look at all these lines! It must have nearly killed him!"

Marcos agreed. "Well, it almost did."

She set the map down and looked at Marcos. "What could be worth doing that to your body?"

Marcos suddenly looked more surprised than scared. "My treasure. Are you blind?"

"Come on, Marcos, don't you think there should be something more?" said Jules. "Something beyond a treasure that would drive a man to that extreme."

Marcos laughed. "Are you insinuating that there could be something of more value than gold?" He arched his eyebrows. Jules didn't reply, but she thought to herself, "We'll see."

The next day they were on the trail again. The high walls had merged into each other, blocking the way ahead. But a dark hole at the cliff base turned out to be a long, low tunnel that allowed access to the next section.

The tunnel was filled with dark, motionless water. About fifty feet beyond the entrance a bright light marked the exit on the other side.

Marcos began to unbutton his shirt. "We will have to wade through this. Carry anything you don't want to get wet over your head."

Jules started to get undressed and noticed Marcos staring. "Hey, Professor," she said, "Mind your own business."

She finally stepped into the cold water in her bra and underwear, clasping a bundle of clothes and pack to the top of her head.

Marcos watched her from behind.

In the tunnel the cold water was waist deep. They entered the darkness and Marcos turned on a flashlight. He was breathing heavily against the cold of the water. Jules was silent.

Marcos had a hard time using the flashlight while he carried his gear over his head. As its beam swept the ceiling he saw that it was covered with bats. He also noticed symbols scratched into the wall and moved to get a closer look.

Amazed, he said, "Well, look at this..."

Jules was left in the dark, and she called for him to shine her some light.

Feeling unduly distracted from his discovery, Marcos shouted, "SILENCE!"

Suddenly the entire cave was filled with motion. Bats flew everywhere.

Instinctively, Jules and Marcos shielded their faces, and several splashes marked their belongings dropping into the water.

They frantically waded toward the light of the exit.

* * *

Fernando emerged from the tunnel exit with his belongings held over his head, set inside his breastplate. Behind him bats flew in confusion.

He ignored them.

After climbing out of the water, he lay back against a flat rock. His dripping clothes slowly dried; breathing deeply, he enjoyed the warm sunshine.

When he closed his eyes, he thought he could hear someone singing, very softly. He opened them slightly and looked around, but saw nothing and closed them again.

A dull thud hit his shoulder, immediately followed by a sharp pain. An arrow pierced his flesh, and he screamed. His eyes scanned the cliff tops in panic; he could see Indians scampering to get a better shot. Up top, Bidzill announced proudly that it was his arrow that hit the Spaniard.

Arrows landed all around Fernando as he scurried for cover. He stumbled, and almost fell, when another one notched his leg.

"Puta," he screamed.

He huddled behind a jumble of boulders and took out his guns. He had a black powder rifle and pistol, but the wounded shoulder didn´t allow for the quick, military precision with which he usually loaded them.

The Indians began to attack, led by Bidzill. Aditsan was also with them, although he lagged behind.

Moving like ghosts down the slopes of the canyon, they closed the distance quickly.

Bidzill taunted Aditsan, "This is your chance to be a man, Aditsan. Come with me."

Aditsan followed, but looked miserable. While Bidzill yelled at him again, two other warriors took the lead. Bidzill glared at Aditsan.

"If you cost me his scalp I will beat you," he threatened. Aditsan stepped up his pace.

The other warriors reached Fernando just as he finished loading the rifle. He shot one in the stomach and turned to locate another coming from behind. He killed him with the pistol.

There was smoke everywhere. The remaining Indians retreated, melting into the rocks.

Fernando snuck around a rock to the Indian with the stomach wound who stood against a boulder, moaning. He pulled out a large knife and finished him off. He grinned fiercely as he threw the body to the earth.

After grabbing his gear Fernando limped up the canyon, scanning the environment for the enemy. He didn't see the Indians who were silently pursuing him.

Chapter Five

Marcos and Jules sat on opposite sides of a fire. They were both wearing only their underwear, with damp coats over their shoulders to keep their backs warm.

Marcos was shivering, despite almost leaning into the flame. The soaking seemed to have humbled him.

Jules seemed to take some satisfaction from his miserable state. "So, Marcos, is this how you envisioned your great discovery?" she asked.

He laughed. "Not exactly, but I do have a contingency plan." He pulled a bottle of brandy out of his backpack and took a swig.

He gestured to her. "This will warm you up." Jules took the bottle and choked down a swallow.

"You seem pretty comfortable here. Has your family been in Arizona long?"

Jules smiled at the question. "My father was from Montana, but my mom was local," said Jules. "She was Indian—her people claim to have been created here."

"You mean they arrived a few thousand years ago?" asked Marcos.

"Some would argue much longer," replied Jules.

"I'm sorry to disappoint you," said Marcos. "But your ancestors came from Asia, and before that Mesopotamia. They were not created here."

Jules stared at the fire for a minute before replying. "Well even if they weren't created here, they took their identity from this place."

Marcos gave her a disdainful sigh.

"Those are two very different things," said Marcos. "Well, it's good to know I've got an Indian guide, even if she does believe in fairy tales."

She took another swig and handed the bottle back.

As he lifted the bottle to his lips, she asked, "So how is it that you have this map, but don't know where the treasure actually is?"

He choked and struggled to quench a cough.

* * *

Antonio appeared onto a bald red rock, leading his mule down the large canyon. A sudden storm had just ended, and the sun was out.

He reached the fork where he had separated from his brother, and gasped as he saw Fernando on the ground, battered beyond belief. Antonio let go of his mule and ran to him.

"Brother, what has become of you?" he demanded.

Fernando was weak, but conscious. He replied, "There is no time, open my shirt."

Antonio did and was horrified at what he saw.

He asked, "Fernando, who did this?"

Fernando almost smiled at the question, and then wincingly pulled a piece of soft leather from his belt. When he opened it with shaking fingers a gold coin fell to the ground.

Fernando looked at the symbol on the top of the piece of leather, and then placed the leather over his chest and padded it down, moaning, his breathing heavy with pain.

He grabbed Antonio's shirt, panting, and pleaded, "You must go back for me Antonio. I was a fool. Use the map."

Antonio was breathless, "What map? Tell me what you found!"

Before he could reply the canyon filled with the faint sound of singing. They both froze. A gust of wind blew through, and then the singing was gone.

Antonio shook himself. "What is this witchcraft?"

Fernando moaned loudly, and pulled his brother to him.

He whispered something into Antonio's ear, and then slumped back. Whether he had just lost consciousness or was dead, Antonio was not sure.

Antonio looked down at the gold coin. He picked it up, and looked at his brother, unsure of what to do.

He then stared at the leather stuck to Fernando's chest. Squeamishly, he lifted it, and examined it. It all seemed to be a bit much for him.

Nervously, he rubbed the back of his neck.

Robert DeMayo

The sun had come up, but the floor of the narrow canyon still lay in the shadows. High up in the cliffs the Indians watched, looking for signs of the Spaniard.

Grey Wolf was chanting over a low fire. There was a large chunk of meat roasting over the coals.

He had Fernando's armor and was working it with his knife as Aditsan approached. He looked over his grandson, noticed a welt over one eye, and asked, "Did the Spaniard do that?"

Aditsan looked away. "No, this was a punishment." Grey Wolf nodded that he understood, but he didn't look happy.

Then Aditsan turned back and smiled, everything forgotten, as he said, "Grandfather, I have met a girl."

Grey Wolf smiled. "I did not know there was anyone new in the tribe. Who are her parents?"

"I do not know," replied Aditsan. "I only saw her this morning, by the west fork." Grey Wolf's eyes became serious, but he acted relaxed.

"You know the witch's canyon is taboo, and it is somewhere up the west fork," he said.

Aditsan grinned, because this was an old argument with them. "No one knows where the witch lives, so how can I fear it?"

The old chief persisted, very seriously: "It is not a place for men. If you ever find it, stay out."

He cut a piece off the cooking mule meat and handed it to Aditsan. "Eat some meat. If the Spaniard does leave the canyon he will have to walk."

Bidzill had walked up, hearing Grey Wolf's words, and stated, "He will not leave; and I will not eat again until he is dead."

"You should not make vows where the witch can hear you," Grey Wolf replied.

"I'm not afraid of your witch," said Bidzill. "I have said I will kill her as well."

Grey Wolf turned away. "They should have named you Eskaminzim, Big Mouth."

Bidzill was offended. "How can we let the Spaniard dishonor us? He has killed two of our men. For this he must die."

"From the beginning I advised you to stay away from the home of the witch," stated Grey Wolf.

Bidzill looked away and refused to reply.

Grey Wolf reached forward and gently grabbed Bidzill's wrist. "I see you are ruled by anger now, but there will come a time when that ends."

Bidzill listened earnestly, hoping the wise chief would offer good advice.

"The witch has not harmed you," continued Grey Wolf. "Forget the witch. Go for the Spaniard, for he has proven to be an enemy. Leave the witch alone."

Confused emotions clouded Bidzill's face as he walked off.

Grey Wolf turned back to Aditsan.

With a smile, he said, "So you met a new girl and you want to impress her."

Aditsan nodded enthusiastically.

Grey Wolf grew solemn, then said, "To make sure no one is offended you must leave an offering. There is no other way."

The old Indian then slid over the Spaniard's breast plate. He placed on it a pile of tiny wires that he had extracted from the plate and bent into hooks. These he poured into a soft leather pouch.

"You must leave this bag where your friend will find it," said Grey Wolf and handed the pouch to Aditsan.

Aditsan took the pouch and tied it to his waist. Then the old chief added, "And you must be near water if you hope not to fall under her spell."

Bidzill had meanwhile walked to the cliff's edge. He peered down and examined a dark recess in the base of the cliff. Then he moved on.

In the dark recess, hidden in the shadows, Fernando watched Bidzill leave. The arrow was still lodged in his shoulder, but he had broken off most of the protruding part.

Fernando was shivering, and he was pale. His guns were laid out beside him.

From his hiding spot he could see a bend in the canyon, cluttered by a pileup of large dead logs.

Nothing moved.

Fernando felt nausea, pain and fatigue overwhelm him. He passed out.

The sound of a large raven´s wings cutting through the air as it landed on one of the logs on the pileup disturbed the silence.

The raven cried out as it did a strange dance, waking Fernando.

He sat up, moaning.

Suddenly, an Indian woman appeared from within a hollow log. She moved slowly, with caution, and she seemed strangely childlike.

Tied to a strand of the young woman's hair, suspended on her forehead, was a small, circular abalone shell, the concave side facing out.

She smiled as she looked directly at Fernando. Then motioned for him to remain hidden, and looked around suspiciously.

Quietly, like a cat, she stepped forward and lifted a string. On its end struggled a large trout.

She grinned.

Suddenly, the canyon filled with the sound of rocks tumbling off the cliff and crashing down into the shadows.

Quickly she hid in the log again.

Bidzill had descended to the canyon floor, Aditsan behind him. He walked straight toward the log and pulled out an arrow.

He screamed, "Witch!"

He flipped the log to expose her, and then staggered backward, seemingly afraid of her. At the same time Aditsan saw the girl and instantly recognized her as the one he'd seen that morning.

He screamed, "NO!"

Aditsan grabbed Bidzill's arm to stop him, but Bidzill spun with a vicious punch that knocked Aditsan out. Turning to the woman again, he notched his arrow.

A raven dropped out of the sky and attacked him.

It swooped at him repeatedly. Bidzill fought it off, gasping in surprise, and finally watched it fly away.

Then he turned to the woman again, notched an arrow and prepared to shoot.

Suddenly, the thunderous "bam!" of a muzzle loader echoed through the canyon and Bidzill fell forward. The sound was so loud it felt otherworldly.

A line of smoke led from Bidzill's body to Fernando, who stood a short distance away, the sun reflecting off his helmet.

He looked feverish and unsteady.

He stumbled toward the unconscious Aditsan with his knife out for the kill. The Indian woman moved fast and in a split-second stood between them protectively.

He looked at her, confused, and then collapsed at her feet.

She knelt, lay his arm around her neck to pick him up, and with difficulty carried him to the shadows.

His rifle was left behind.

Out of sight, in the shadows at the base of the cliff, the Indian woman looked at the unconscious Fernando.

She spoke out loud, like she was used to talking to herself.

"I could not let you kill him," she said.

She removed his helmet, and examined it, amazed by the way it reflected light.

Laughing quietly, she touched his face, and said, "He will be your undoing."

She heard something, scanned the cliff tops, and then froze.

A moment later, an Indian appeared running along a trail on the edge of the canyon rim. The morning sun highlighted his hurry, and she could clearly see him scanning the canyon floor.

In a moment he was gone.

The Indian woman continued to drag Fernando further up the canyon, always staying in the shadows.

"They will not find us where we go," she said to the unconscious man.

Finally, Fernando came around.

He struggled to get on his feet and staggered along with her help; his focus coming and going.

They made it to the top of a short scree and she ushered Fernando behind a large rock.

A moment later she returned to cover up their trail, and then disappeared behind the rock again.

Robert DeMayo

The raven was also there. He sat perched on the rock for a moment, like a sentinel, and then disappeared as well.

Chapter Six

Marcos and Jules followed the creek upstream; the sun was shining through the trees and the canyon air was cool.

Jules came up behind Marcos, and asked," So you don't know what he found?"

Marcos grinned wide and said, "Isn't it obvious?"

Jules did not reply.

"He had an Aztec coin on him," said Marcos. "Possibly the very coin I found 300 years later."

He shook his head in disbelief.

Jules was still skeptical. "Possibly" she repeated. "What did he say?"

"What did who say?" replied Marcos.

"What did Fernando say to his brother right before he passed out?" asked Jules. "You said he whispered something."

Marcos missed a step and almost fell.

"I didn't say he whispered something," he said defensively. "His brother told him to go back for the treasure."

Jules glared at him, "You're lying."

Robert DeMayo

He puffed up. "You have no right to any information leading to my treasure."

"You're an asshole," said Jules. "And you know where you can stick your treasure."

Jules stepped swiftly past him and took the lead which annoyed Marcos even more. They stopped when they saw a small stream trickling in on their right. Marcos scratched his head. "We have gone too far."

Jules studied the map, "But that's impossible. There have been no exits."

"I agree with you," said Marcos, "but according to my map we have gone too far."

"You sure you got the right canyon Marcos?"

He glared at her, and she added, "Maybe you're holding the map upside-down."

His face flushed red. "We are in the right place."

They turned around and start walking downstream.

Finally Marcos stopped again and looked around, confused. Jules took off her pack, "I'm sick of this. We've been going back and forth for hours."

"Go home if you want. I don't need you," said Marcos.

"Lighten up, Marcos. I'm just saying I can't see any other ways out of this canyon."

Marcos dropped his pack, "I agree, and it's getting late. I know we are close, but we should make camp."

He pulled out the tent. They set it up, and made camp in silence.

Later, in the tent, they had their heads at opposite ends. Marcos had the tent unzipped, his head by the entrance. He twitched in his sleep, seemingly reliving his nightmare once again.

Jules kicked his sleeping bag, "Hey Professor, zip up the tent." He didn't move; he had mosquitoes on his forehead.

Jules stared into space, lost in thought; and then pulled her bag over her head for protection.

Jules flashed back to the visit to the reservation with her father. She remembered sitting up in bed, waiting patiently when her father finally entered the room.

She jumped out of bed, ran to him and wrapped her arms around him, like she used to, and asked, "Dad, I want to ask you to do something . . . something difficult."

Her embrace warmed him, and he replied, "Anything girl. What's on your mind?"

Jules let him go and stared at the floor while she collected her thoughts. "Auntie wants me to participate in the next Changing Woman ceremony. She's says I'm the right age."

Her father stepped away from her, "That crazy old witch? I really don't want you to get mixed up in all that stuff."

Jules stood her ground, "Mom didn't think it was crazy. She liked it here—they all still talk about her."

He stiffened, and looked down at his daughter, "Well she's not here to defend herself."

59

Jules stared at the floor again. "Or me," she said quietly.

"I think it's just best if we dropped it."

Jules pleaded, "You know Mom wanted this for me! And you didn't mind it when she was alive!"

George smiled benevolently, "But I know better now. Those are just stories, Jules, they're not real."

Jules shook her head, "No, Auntie told me there is truth in them. She wants to teach me the old ways like mom wanted."

George shook his head firmly, "I'm sorry Jules, you have to just have faith in Jesus . . . when we get home we should all have a good talk with father Frank."

She climbed back into bed, and pulled the covers up to her chin. "I don't want to talk to father Frank! I want to do this."

George pulled a small Bible out of his pocket and held it up for assurance. His voice had become stern. "When you are on your own you can go off chasing these false prophets, but while under my roof you are going to follow the one true faith."

Almost to herself, she said, "It'll be too late then, Auntie will be gone."

"I put up with this nonsense while your mother was alive," George said loudly. "Now it's time to let it go!"

Jules remained silent while she stared at her father, but thought to herself, "When I'm older, I'll come back without you. I'll come back and find that cave, just like my mother did."

The Cave Where The Water Always Drips

* * *

Three bodies lay motionless on the canyon floor. The Indian woman that had saved Fernando appeared silently and moved from one to the next.

A faint scent of gunpowder still hung in the air, mixing with the smell of the pines. She moved with stealth, and kept to the shadows whatever possible.

She paused next to Aditsan when she saw he was still alive. She knelt down and gave him some water. Slowly he stirred as she raised his head and applied a wet cloth to the swollen area where he was punched.

He groaned in pain.

She took a single eagle down feather that was tied to the back of her hair and tied it to a strand of his hair. He was barely aware, his vision blurred.

She smiled at him, and said, "I remember you." He stared at her, struggling to fully come to.

She added, "I knew I would see you again."

She wet his forehead again and he blinked away the water and sunshine.

"By the creek, in the morning light," she said softly, "you seemed so beautiful that it frightened me and I ran away. I have been alone too long."

Then she kissed him, long, until she sensed he was awakening; as his eyes started moving she jumped up, giggling.

"And I will not forget that you tried to save me either," she said with a smile.

She walked toward the wall of the canyon and disappeared into a grove of junipers.

He lifted himself on his elbows and stared after her, shaken.

The Indian woman and Fernando were in a small, steep-walled canyon with no apparent outlets. It was about forty feet wide and at least twice as long, narrowing near the cliffs along the back wall.

 The far end rose a little, and was lost in a grove of ghostly sycamore trees.

Fernando was unconscious.

The Indian woman stood with her back to the stone wall and faced east.

She now wore a spectacularly fringed, buckskin dress. It was decorated with bells and beads. Despite her youth, there was something ancient in her appearance.

She was motionless, her eyes closed, until a shaft of light plunged over the canyon rim and struck the abalone shell on her forehead.

Then she began to jump up and down, dancing in place. The small bells on her dress tinkled.

She started to chant.

Fernando stirred and opened his eyes slightly.

He could not follow her words, but saw her point to herself and repeat something over and over as she chanted, "Kamalapukwia, Kamalapukwia, Kamalapukwia..."

He pleaded for help, believing the strange word to be her name, "Kamala, por favor."

She stopped and smiled at this and walked to him.

After kneeling and standing three times, she sprinkled pollen on his head.

He was fading again as she produced a straight, yellow, drinking tube and sucked up some liquid from a bowl.

She then leaned forward, opened his mouth and spit the liquid into it. He passed out.

Days later, Fernando came to again. He tried to sit up; the Indian woman rushed to his side and set him back.

He looked at her, and thought for a minute. "Kamala?" he asked.

She nodded, and said, "You are safe. They will not enter." But he didn't understand her words.

His shoulder was bandaged, and there was something heavy and solid packed inside the bandage.

He tried to sit up again and winced.

Kamala laughed and it echoed off the walls.

Fernando seemed concerned that the Indians would hear her. He tried to hush her, which made her laugh harder. He tried an Indian word for, "quiet," but she only stared at him, uncomprehending.

She laughed lightly, and then she started to sing.

It was a beautiful, wordless melody which rose up through the surrounding canyons, echoing.

Fernando tried to stop her again, "Do dah Ha'do'aal," he said. "Don´t sing!"

It stopped her for a minute. She stared at him, started to laugh, and then repeated his words, "Do dah Ha'do'aal?"

He nodded.

She laughed, and started singing again.

This time louder.

Far up on the canyon rim, Grey Wolf lifted his head to the sound. It was impossible to tell which direction it came from, the words coming and going with the wind.

One of the younger warriors closed his eyes and began to sway to her song, then jerked himself conscious, afraid, as if he had just been bewitched.

Grey Wolf grinned.

In another canyon, Aditsan heard it as well. He seemed desperate to know its source. He walked to a still pool of water, and lowered his ear to listen.

What came to him was a clearer sound, but no direction.

Turning his head, he caught his reflection in the water, and for the first time saw the eagle-down feather tied there.

Chapter Seven

Kamala squatted next to Fernando to feed him fish stew from a small clay bowl.

As she leaned close, she said, "Fish."

Fernando repeated the word, "Fish."

Kamala smiled, "It is worth leaving the canyon for fish; and normally there is no one else there."

The raven landed between them and cried out loudly. Kamala brushed it away, and said, "He is jealous. Before you came he was my only friend. "

She looked down, sadly, as she stirred the stew, and added, "I have been alone."

The raven cawed as if insulted.

Fernando eyed him with distrust.

Then he tossed a small rock at the bird, making it hop out of the way. Kamala said, "Earlier I thought you were a God. Now I do not know."

The raven cried out again.

"He does not think you are," said Kamala.

"We will see. If you are only a man then you've come to a bad place—at least for men."

Kamala appeared, now wearing a simpler buckskin skirt. It was plain, but more functional. After placing a clay container near the fire, she checked Fernando's bandages.

"Thank you, Kamala," said Fernando, "I don't know how to thank you for saving me — for helping me escape." There was true affection in his eyes.

She understood some of his words, but ignored them. He was still weak, and for now her patient, but she still didn't trust him.

He tried again to see what the solid thing was that was bundled over his wound, inside his shirt.

As she had done earlier, she pushed his hand away, warning him. "That medicine is the only reason you are still alive, but if you even look at it you will be doomed."

Fernando leaned back and smiled casually. All he understood of her reply was a warning. When she was not looking he dug into the bandages again.

But Kamala caught it, whacked him with a cooking spoon and moved away, laughing.

Fernando laughed as well, but once she was out of sight his smile vanished.

He groaned while he unbuttoned his shirt and pulled out his pistol. After checking it over thoroughly he put it away.

He looked around slowly, assessing the place.

Soundlessly, Kamala made her way to the edge of the creek. In the pre-dawn light she moved like a creature of the forest. Patiently, she searched through the dew-covered grass until she found a grasshopper and tied it, with difficulty, to her line.

It struggled on the water's surface and then quickly disappeared. She smiled as she pulled up a trout.

After dropping it into a leather bag, she took one quick look around and departed.

Twenty paces away Aditsan stood. He moved to where she sat and examined the spot. The rock was still warm to the touch from her body heat.

He then took the small bundle Grey Wolf had given him and opened it to reveal the fish hooks made from the Spanish wire.

With reverence he placed the package in the open, by the water's edge, and walked off in the direction she took — searching the ground for tracks as he went.

Fernando was sleeping, Kamala was nowhere in sight. The raven hopped over to him until he was only inches from his face.

It put its beak forward, all but touching his eye, and stared at him.

Kamala appeared at the stream's edge and cupped a drink. She took out her string, and then a hook made from Spanish wire.

While she tied the hook to the line she smiled.

With stealth she caught a grasshopper and tossed the baited line into the water.

She was sure she was alone—until Aditsan gently grabbed her wrist from behind. He had been there for hours, concealed, as if he were waiting for an eagle to land.

For a moment she looked panicked, but quickly Aditsan dipped his hand in the creek and flicked some water in her face.

Surprised, she smiled broadly.

"I will not harm you," Aditsan said,

She gently touched his wound to see if it was healing. He smelled her hair when she came close.

He said, "I saw you before, by the creek..."

Kamala smiled and put her fingers over his lips to silence him.

Slowly they lay back on the warm rocks and embraced. Aditsan couldn't believe his luck.

Kamala emerged up out of a hole by the base of the wall. By her side she held a string of fish.

Fernando was standing with his bandages loosely strung around him. In his hands he held the heavy object that was in his bandage.

Kamala glared at him, "Why are all men so predictable?"

Fernando didn't hear her. His eyes were riveted to a White Stone that he had just pulled from his bandages.

The Cave Where The Water Always Drips

The stone was the shape of a flattened softball. It was pure white, with a band of gold inlaid. Hammered into the gold were Aztec symbols.

Fernando was shaking, almost hyperventilating, as he coarsely asked, "Where did you get this?"

"It comes from a place that will bring you no good," warned Kamala.

He reached for his gun, and belted out, "Bring me to this treasure."

She tried to calm him, but he backhanded her.

Almost immediately there was a flash of lightning and the crash of thunder. It echoed over and over throughout the surrounding canyons.

Fernando stepped back in fear, and looked around.

The raven landed next to Kamala and watched him, and then started to caw loudly and repeatedly. The echoes of the raven´s call mixed strangely with the thunder.

The sky had darkened.

Fernando whispered, "Great mother of God."

* * *

Jules awoke from a dream and exited the tent without waking Marcos. Outside, a full moon shone down on the canyon, making the sycamore trees look alive.

She looked around, not certain what force had called her from slumber.

Far off she could hear coyotes howling.

Robert DeMayo

Suddenly something buzzed past her head, and
landed a few feet away. A large raven stood looking at
her, defiantly.

"I remember you," said Jules. "You owe me for the
parking lot."

It hopped around, making strange gurgling noises,
and stared. Jules eyed it for a minute, and then said,
"Don't plan on getting any treats from me if you scare
me again."

It tilted its head sideways, and finally flew up a
nearby scree and disappeared behind a large rock at the
cliff base.

Jules watched for several minutes, but it never
reappeared. She climbed the scree.

Behind the rock was a small tunnel that lead up;
obviously the course of a stream during the rainy
season. The tunnel was a mere ten feet long; moonlight
flooded the other side.

Jules climbed through the tunnel and emerged into a
box canyon. There was no wind; it was dead silent, and
time seemed to have stopped. The moon cast disturbing
shadows everywhere.

Something by the wall reflected the moonlight and
Jules headed that way, each of her steps echoing off the
high walls.

By a crumbling adobe wall sat a Spanish helmet. It
was set on a large flat rock, as if on display. Jules

reached to touch it, but stopped mid-way when she thought she heard a woman singing.

Motionlessly, she listened; she was barely breathing, her heart pounded. And then she heard the faint song, with a melody that held her in a trance.

And just as quickly it was gone.

Jules prided herself that she did not fear many things; she was calm when many of her friends wanted to run—but the singing woman spooked her, and she looked around fearfully.

After a moment she retreated.

As she climbed backward through the tunnel, her eyes never left the canyon, as if she might expect someone to follow her. She returned to the tent and silently crawled into her bag.

The quietness of the next morning was shattered by Marcos´s screams. He burst through the zippered fly of the tent like he was escaping from the demons of Hell.

Jules figured it was just another nightmare until he kicked free of his sleeping bag, and started pointing.

"There's something in my bag," he shrieked. He shook his leg, and then touched his calf.

"I think it bit me," he added.

Jules lifted the sleeping bag and shook it.

A rattlesnake hit the ground and slithered away. Marcos cried, "There, I told you."

Jules grabbed her pack and fetched a small medical kit.

"I told you to shut the flap," she calmly said.

She pointed at his leg, and added, "Take off your pants. Let me look." Marcos took them off; there was a single puncture mark.

"There is only one puncture," said Jules, "it looks like it was a glancing blow." She handed his pants back, and added, "You might get lucky, but we should start back right away, regardless."

"That's ridiculous," Marcos snapped. "I am not going anywhere. My treasure is here, I can feel it."

Jules sighed. "You stupid man, I can't carry you all the way back."

He started shouting. "I am not leaving! Go if you want; I don't need you!"

Jules just said, "There's nothing here for you."

Marcos stared at her for a long minute. Then he narrowed his eyes and said, "You're hiding something."

Jules said nothing. Her gaze was directed toward the scree and the tunnel. Marcos noticed it.

As he started heading in the direction of her stare, he saw her footprints leading up the hill.

He flared up, "Is this why you want me to leave?" He took a step toward her, his face contorted in anger.

"You found something!" he screamed and swung his arm as if to strike. But something stopped him.

Instead, he angrily jabbed his finger at her. "You have no right to it!"

Then he stumbled up the hill, behind the rock. Jules took a breath and followed.

Chapter Eight

On the Colorado Plateau a low fire burned in a ponderosa pine forest. A leg of an Elk sizzled over the fire, and behind Antonio on the ground lay the rest of the carcass.

Antonio grinned as he cut off a chunk of meat.

"Fernando," he said, "if you could see how well I live now."

He chewed with relish until a sharp "crack" startled him, and he saw movement in the shadows. He grabbed his rifle with shaking hands.

The blood had drained from his face, sweat formed on his brow.

A lone coyote came into view. It was limping.

Antonio puffed out his breath and relaxed. "You won't make it long with that leg," he said to the coyote and tossed him a piece of meat.

It quickly snatched the meat out of the air and disappeared.

Grey Wolf watched the scene from the darkness.

He observed Antonio feeding the coyote with amusement, but when he saw the elk carcass on the ground behind him he shook his head.

He backed away and talked to a brave who accompanied him.

Grey Wolf said, "This one will be lucky to survive at all. We will leave him."

Later, Antonio leaned back and crossed his arms behind his head.

Suddenly a dark shadow hovered over him. He spun around to see the massive head of a Grizzly as it sank its teeth into the Elk carcass.

It stared at Antonio for a minute, from only a foot away, and then the bear and the carcass all disappeared into the night.

Antonio turned white and started to shake.

He cried softly, "Brother, where are you?"

Fernando ran around the box canyon, flipping stones and searching any crevice he could find. He was laughing, almost hysterically, despite the fact that he found nothing.

Next he dug through Kamala's possessions, and the sheltered area near a fire pit. She watched silently, the raven on her shoulder.

Slowly he accepted the fact that it was not there.

He glared at her, and she smiled back.

Fernando pulled out his pistol and walked to her. He pointed it at her face and screamed, "Where is it?"

She touched the gun barrel, her eyes full of curiosity.

She asked, "Will you make thunder now?"

He shouted, "Will you not be serious?"

Her laughter drove him insane.

She looked him in the eye, "Guns show a lack of faith; they won't save you."

His gaze slid past her and saw the grove of trees at the far end of the canyon. He ran that way, and Kamala followed.

Between two large trunks was the entrance to a cave, but the other trees were so numerous that it took a bit of maneuvering before Fernando got there.

There was just enough daylight to show a dim chamber.

Kamala stood by the entrance, blocking his way. "This cave is not for men — only women go there."

He pushed her out of the way, but had difficulty squeezing through the trees to get to the cave entrance.

Kamala warned him again, "People who go beyond these trees must have a pure heart — not everyone can enter."

Again, he laughed at her and forced an entrance.

In a last attempt, she pleaded with him. "Do not go inside, Fernando."

Inside, the cave was low, damp, and only about five feet high. Water dripped all around them, echoing.

It was dark.

Fernando frantically searched for another chamber, but found none—only a twenty-five foot diameter area.

In the center of the cave was a small, sandy rise covered with a pile of offerings. The water did not drip here and it was dry.

Fernando rushed to the pile and started pawing through it. Kamala grabbed him from behind and tried to stop him.

His eyes were all over the cave as he dug into the sand mound. "I know the treasure is near!"

He held up a hand-made doll in disbelief, "What is this rubbish?"

Kamala grabbed it from him and tried to steer him away.

He turned and smacked her.

A drop of blood flew from her face onto the sand.

They wrestled, and he rolled on top of her. Her youthful, near-naked form underneath him turned his anger and he started tearing off her clothing.

It started to pour outside.

She screamed, but the sound was lost in the booming of thunder. "Is this what I saved you for?" she asked between her clenched teeth.

The lightning beyond the cave entrance was now blinding. She fought like an animal, biting and punching at every opportunity, but he didn't relent.

Bleeding and scratched, he eventually overwhelmed her.

When he had finished he left the cave.

Kamala remained on her back, sobbing, staring at the cave ceiling, only a few feet above her. Eventually she wiped her face and sat up, aching.

Slowly her emotions hardened.

She looked at her hand and noticed it was smeared with blood. Looking up at the ceiling, she made a red handprint.

The raven landed next to her and stared.

She addressed the raven, "His days are numbered. He will be gone soon."

The raven just stared; it didn't seem to need to blink.

"Why do you think I brought him to our canyon?" she added, "He will bring it upon himself, don't worry, this is not a place for men."

* * *

Jules climbed the narrow hole that lead up into the box canyon to find Marcos staring in awe.

He talked reverently as he surveyed the box canyon, "This is it. My treasure is here."

Jules looked around suspiciously.

At the far end of the canyon was a mass of rotted logs; to the left, a ruined adobe structure, and not much else. It appeared to be a dead end as the walls all ran straight up.

Marcos approached the ruins and spotted the Spanish helmet. He picked it up and displayed it to Jules. He had that manic look of pride on his face again.

"My ancestor."

Then he started to run around like an idiot, searching everywhere, and soon, he began to limp. He was on the verge of passing out when Jules convinced him to sit down.

He glared at her, "You knew it was here."

She ignored his words, "You're gonna need a doctor."

Marcos sneered at her, "You just want me to leave so you can get my treasure."

Jules looked around, but didn't say anything.

"I don't trust you," he added.

She remained quiet as she approached him to tie a bandanna around his leg, just above the snake bite. As he watched her do this his eyes were cold and focused.

"There's snakeweed here," said Jules. "I've heard you can make a poultice to put on the bite that might help." He was sarcastic in his reply, "Look who's suddenly an Indian. Did your mother raise you as a medicine woman?"

She walked away, "Let it rot off. I don't care."

"That's what I thought," replied Marcos.

"You'd like me to die so you could have it all."

She was annoyed with him, and said, "How much treasure can you carry out with one leg anyway?"

Marcos became serious.

He looked at her, but said nothing. Jules began to collect the snakeweed and process it.

The tent was set up, and a fire was smoldering in a pit by the ruined adobe structure. Marcos and Jules sat with their backs to the wall as they waited for the sun to peak over the high cliffs.

Marcos had the snakeweed poultice on his calf.

Slowly the light descended, illuminating the cliff wall dramatically. Suddenly Marcos jumped up, and shouted, "Do you see that?"

Jules looked up expectantly. "See what?"

Marcos limped over to the wall, and pointed, "Here! Look! There is a vertical line of holes drilled into this rock face."

Jules looked, but her face was still skeptical, "Are you sure it's man-made?"

Marcos was rapidly losing his patience with her, and snapped, "Of course it is. Look at the precision."

Each hole was about an inch wide, deeper than a finger, and two feet above the last.

He proudly pointed to the holes. "This is a ladder."

Jules laughed, "Are you high? Where would it go to?" They both looked up the wall, but all they could see from the ground was fifty vertical feet. Further up, the cliff slanted back.

Marcos replied, as if it should have been obvious, "It goes up. They put the treasure up there."

He started to walk in circles, mumbling as he made his plan.

"We will make pegs," he said, "and place them in the holes, and climb."

Jules looked over the holes, and then looked all the way up. "You're on your own, Marcos."

He rolled his eyes. "You are a coward."

Jules shook her head, "I don't think the treasure is up there, and I'm not going near your so-called ladder."

He shrugged it off, "I do not need your help. You have no rights to this treasure anyway." She sighed and replied, "You're gonna break your damn neck."

Marcos stormed off searching for sticks.

Whenever he had the opportunity, he glared at Jules. When he had collected an armful he sat against the wall, took out a big knife and started making pegs.

He was pretty worked up, and made it a point of focusing his frustration on Jules.

"You could have been famous," said Marcos.

He chopped a long stick in half, and added, "You could have been part of restoring my family honor."

He hacked at another stick.

Jules looked at the distance up the cliff again.

"No, I'd rather just watch this." Marcos stopped working and looked at her for a long time.

"Yes, I can see this now," stated Marcos. "Family honor doesn't mean anything to you."

Jules stared at the ground.

Marcos continued, "You have nothing to say? Why aren't you telling me how proud you are of your people? Or your family? How about your tribe?"

She snapped back, "What's so great about people, Marcos? Or family for that matter."

Marcos smiled and pointed at her with his knife. "That's right, you don't know them. You don't know your ancestors either."

Jules got up and walked away. "Go to hell."

He gave her an evil grin as he drove his point home. "That is why you don't know yourself." He stuck the knife in a log and limped to the wall.

Marcos placed one of his foot-long pegs in a hole and stood on it, testing its strength. Then he inserted another in the next hole.

In this manner he began to climb the cliff face.

"You see, it is so simple," he called.

He moved up a step, and said, "Because you could not conceive it, you shall not share in my great discovery."

Jules replied, "Why not let me worry about what I conceive."

To this Marcos laughed, "One like you is not worthy of my noble bloodline."

Jules leaned against the wall to watch, "Keep climbing, Marcos. This is gonna be good."

Soon he was thirty feet above the ground, but there seemed to be no end to the ascent. The rock face above remained vertical for another twenty feet before slanting back, out of sight.

As he moved to place another peg there was a "crack" and a nervous expression crossed his face.

As he moved to descend, the peg he was standing on snapped and he began to fall.

Frantically he reached for the passing pegs, and managed to grab one, just to have it break and send him crashing through the remainder of the pegs.

He hit the ground hard, only to find it was actually. . .

. . .Fernando, who had tried the same stunt.

Kamala watched with a satisfied grin as he limped to the fire.

The raven cawed and flew off.

As it ascended above the section the men were climbing, it got a bird's overview of everything.

On the flat surface of the wall, out of sight from the box canyon, was a huge Aztec glyph, carved into the rock.

Chapter Nine

Fernando achingly walked to the fire and squatted. Kamala and the raven sat nearby; watching him. In addition to his earlier injuries, he was now covered with scratches from his fight with Kamala.

Kamala was weaving a basket from a pile of yucca leaves. She looked pale and ignored him as he looked up at the sky. He said, "Finally a warm day. We should see the sun soon."

Kamala said nothing.

He tried again, "I'm sorry about what happened in the cave, I should not have taken liberties with you."

Kamala got up and filled a bowl with food. She handed it to him, and then walked away.

"I am of noble blood, pure Spanish," said Fernando. "In Mexico city I am allowed such privileges—with any woman. I know you do not understand, but what we did is considered an honor in many parts of the Spanish empire."

She stared at him with barely concealed hatred.

The raven hopped over and stood by her. Fernando was uncomfortable with the silence.

ROBERT DEMAYO?

Robert DeMayo

He asked, "How did you come to live here alone?"
She stared at the raven before replying.
"When I was young I was brought here for the Changing Woman ceremony," said Kamala. "I was blindfolded, and when I could see I was here with five medicine men."
Fernando moved closer. "Did they tell you of the treasure?" he asked.
Kamala smiled. "They told me of greater things."

Kamala leaned against the wall while repairing Fernando's shirt. He stretched out next to her; his body was a mass of scars and bruises.
He smiled at her, but she ignored him.
"Would you leave this canyon, Kamala?" asked Fernando. "Would you go away with me?"
She stared without answering; Fernando thought she looked a bit sickly.
When she was done with the shirt, she methodically checked his wounds, all without emotion; and then handed him his shirt.
He moaned as he put it back on, and buttoned it.
"What did the medicine men tell you?" he asked.
She stared with mistrust.
"They were wise men," said Kamala. "One knew herbs, one the body, one the blood, one the proper food to eat . . . and one the heart and soul."
She added, "The one that taught matters of the heart said I would one day find love — do you love me

84

Fernando?" Fernando looked away and would not meet her eyes.

She continued, "When the medicine men had finished, an old woman appeared and told me the legend of White Painted Woman."

"She spoke of what life would be like, how to cope with hardships and depression, how to be happy, and how and where to find guidance and protection."

Kamala turned away to fetch something from her supplies. When she did Fernando reached behind his back, grabbed the pistol and stuck it inside his shirt.

She turned to him, and although she couldn't possibly have seen what he did, the look in her eyes said she had.

Fernando approached Kamala as she harvested the pods of a mesquite bush, on the far side of the box canyon. He was covered in mud, and grinning.

She stepped back in apprehension, and dropped her basket. Quickly Fernando knelt and started collecting the contents of the basket.

When he was done refilling it, he said, "Kamala, come with me," and took her hand and led her to the sheltered area by the fire.

She stepped behind him, a bit reluctant, and her eyes on his hand like it was a limb that needed to be chopped.

Next to her cooking area there now stood a simple adobe hut. It was only one room, with two walls; the other walls were formed by a corner in the canyon.

Kamala stepped forward and Fernando proudly nodded, and said, "I have built this for you."

She entered the structure alone.

Inside she inspected the walls until she came across a hidden space near the ceiling.

After a quick glance to make sure Fernando couldn't see, she reached in her dress and pulled out a sharp knife. As fast as a ferret she hid her knife in the hidden space.

When she came out she was smiling.

Fernando put a red flower in her hair.

She stepped forward to hug him, but as she placed her arms around his waist she felt the pistol. She stepped back and eyed him with mistrust.

The raven flew in and landed on her shoulder.

Kamala emerged from the exit tunnel with a basket of sacred datura; the white blossoms looked alive they were so vibrant.

Fernando sat by the fire. He looked exhausted. She looked around and saw he had destroyed most of her possessions in one of his fits.

He pleaded with her, "I'm sorry, Kamala. I can feel that I am near it. It haunts me."

Kamala gave a weak smile, and started processing the sacred datura. As she prepared the tea for Fernando, she ignored the warnings she had been taught about the poisonous and psychedelic properties of the plant.

She said, "I will make you a drink to relax."

Before he could reply she turned, knelt, and got sick. He moved to help her.

She resisted him, but gave in and allowed him to move her to the fire. She abandoned her plans to make the tea.

Kamala leaned against the wall, her eyes focused; she didn't look healthy. On her knees she held a soft piece of leather; she was painting something on it.

On the ground were several piles of powder that she mixed to make paint. She used a frayed stick for a brush.

Quickly stabbing her finger with a thorn, she added a drop of blood to the mix.

Fernando approached and looked at the circular symbol she had just painted on the leather. She handed it to him and smiled, and said, "I am not used to having company."

After a minute she continued, "When the medicine men left, they said they would return in the morning, but they did not."

Fernando sat down next to her.

"A few times over the years I awoke to see one of the Medicine Men standing over me. They looked aged and defeated."

She added, "In the morning they were gone. Sometimes they left food."

After some thought Fernando said, "Maybe something bad happened to your tribe." He thought some more, then added, "It could have been disease, or they could have been attacked."

She shrugged, "I don't know. It was long ago that they visited last. The year must come and go; it is still like that."

He asked, "So you have been alone here all this time?"

Kamala smiled.

She said, "Not at all. Somebody watches me. Somebody hears me. I am not alone."

* * *

Jules woke up in the dead of night. Marcos slept by her side; he twitched in his sleep, but lay undisturbed as she quietly slipped out of her sleeping bag and exited the tent.

The full moon was gone and it was very dark. After a moment her eyes adjusted and she moved away from their campsite, which was now near the adobe ruins.

From the back of the canyon she could hear something that sounded like a chant. The further back in the box canyon she walked, the clearer the sound became.

She stopped in front of a pile of logs, near the cliff wall. As soon as she touched one of the logs the chanting stopped.

Jules climbed on top of several of the logs and moved them. They were rotted, and covered with charcoal from a fire. Behind the debris, she could see a low cave.

It was dark, and sucked the wind in.

Peering into the cave she heard the singing again. It was very faint and came from inside the cave. From this close she could tell the singer was female.

Slowly she moved backwards, away.

How far back the cave went, she could not tell, but the voice she heard did not sound far away. And then it changed back to the chanting again.

The real question was, did she have the courage to enter the cave?

Jules prepared to step into the cave, when the chanting suddenly stopped. The darkness in front of her was so dense it smothered her.

She lost her nerve and turned to go, only to find Marcos standing there — furious.

She shrieked and jumped.

He hissed, "What are you doing here?"

She still hadn't caught her breath. "You bastard, you scared me."

He didn't care. "I said what are you doing here?"

"Will you relax!" said Jules. "I had to go to the bathroom. Can't I get a little privacy?"

Marcos looked around suspiciously. From where he stood the entrance to the cave was just barely visible. In the darkness he missed it.

He said, "I don't trust you. You're being deceitful."

Robert DeMayo

"Lighten up, Marcos," she replied. "I just had to take a leak."

He stood staring at her. "I will have this treasure."

Jules unbuttoned her jeans, and stared back.

"Do you mind?" she asked

He turned and walked away.

Chapter Ten

High on the cliff wall again, Marcos began shouting as he approached the sunlit area, about thirty feet above the ground.

"Perseverance!" he yelled.

He placed a peg and stepped up. "Endurance!"

He inserted another peg. When he stepped up this time he could see the sun.

"Dedication!"

He stopped and looked down, and said, "I'm sure someone like you can't possibly understand ideas like these. I plan to..."

Suddenly, there was a loud "snap," followed by a scream, and then Marcos came crashing through a number of pegs on his way to the ground.

He hit hard, then painfully stood and shook it off. Then he stepped back and looked at the wall in complete disbelief.

After angrily picking up all of his pegs, he walked over to the campsite.

As he threw them on the fire, he turned, and revealed that he was actually…

… Fernando who had given up on the peg ladder idea as well.

Fernando tended to Kamala, who still looked ill. While she slept he brushed her hair out of her eyes. Then he adjusted her clothing so she would be more comfortable.

He seemed at peace.

He said, "I will never forget that you saved me—and I will take care of you now."

Kamala opened her eyes weakly, and said, "You will forget me when you are tempted."

He smiled affectionately, and said, "No, I am a man of honor." Then taking a knife he pricked his thumb, and said, "I make a vow to stay by your side."

While doing this he felt something solid under her shirt. He reached in and pulled out the White Stone.

The sky overhead began to darken.

The thumb he just stuck had a drop of blood on it. When the blood touched the White Stone it began to glow. Kamala opened her eyes, sat up, and reached for the stone.

She cried out, "What are you doing?"

He pushed her away and she fell. At that moment a bolt of lightning hit one of the trees at the back of the canyon.

He stood over her and shouted, "I will be denied no longer; where is my treasure?"

Fernando held the stone over his head. The wind blew in furious gusts. It pulsed with light.

Kamala screamed, "No!"

Fernando's voice turned dead serious. "I will smash it if you don't tell me."

Kamala stood and reached for it, but he held it higher.

"I will break it," he warned

Her eyes were filled with panic, but then a change came over her. She relaxed. She looked in the direction of the cave, and said, "What you seek is in the cave."

Fernando didn't seem to believe her at first. Then he handed the White Stone to her and moved toward the back of the canyon.

For a moment regret flashed over Kamala's face and she called him, "Fernando."

He turned and stared.

She said, "The Old Woman told me that men who enter the cave do not return the same."

He nodded. "I am not afraid."

"You saved me once so I will warn you. It is protected."

He laughed. "I will kill anyone in my way."

Kamala stared at the ground, then met his eyes, and said, "Stay."

He turned and marched to the back of the box canyon.

At the entrance to the cave the lightning strike had set the trees on fire. The heavy rain did nothing to dampen the flames. Through the smoke the interior of the cave was visible.

Fernando grabbed a flaming branch and ran through a tunnel of fire, and into the cave. The dancing flames were reflecting in the puddles, and made it seem like the cave itself was on fire.

Holding the torch in front of him, he walked the chamber´s perimeter. The ceiling was low, and he leaned forward as he was searching.

While splashing through the puddles he raved, "I pray you are not lying to me, Kamala."

Smoke from the fire outside was slowly filling the cave. He took out his pistol and checked it.

"You Indians may fear witches," said Fernando. "But you will soon learn to fear lead."

As he passed a dark recess, the flame from his torch got sucked away in a howl.

"There!" he shouted.

He stuck the torch into the recess to find it was actually a low tunnel. He moved into it. The tunnel was barely four feet tall and polished smooth.

As it curved to the right he disappeared.

There was a whipping sound, and then a thud.

Fernando screamed.

After a minute he said in a weak voice, "Blood of Christ."

* * *

Marcos stood, leaning against the cliff wall, a short way from the fire. He was unshaven, and his bruises were yellowing.

Jules had a pan of water heating over the fire, and looked busy; but from the corner of her eyes, she kept a close watch on him.

He limped to the fire, trying to look calm.

Smiling broadly, he said, "I can tell when you hide something."

He wagged his finger at her. "I'm not sure why you wouldn't want me to find my treasure," Marcos continued. "I'm not even sure if *you* want to find it."

He picked up the Spanish helmet and stared at it. "But you know something and you don't want to share."

Jules took the pan off the fire and added some freeze-dried food. She ignored him while she stirred it all together.

Marcos said, "You can trust me. I'm a respected professor. I have tenure."

She remained silent.

Exasperated, he turned his palms up, and pleaded, "Please, where is my treasure?"

Jules handed him a bowl of soup.

He took it, lifted the spoon to his mouth and pretended to taste it.

"Why won't you just tell me?" he asked.

He was starting to twitch with frustration.

Jules stood directly in front of him and demanded, "Tell me what Fernando said to Antonio just before he died."

Marcos smashed the bowl of soup against the cliff wall. He seemed to grow in size as he stomped around and angrily yelled at her, "Why can't you just answer a simple question? Are you really so afraid of trusting someone?"

The last question had a visible effect on Jules. She tried to speak, but couldn't find the words. Finally she shrugged it off, and fired back, "Screw it. You want to see where this is all leading?"

Marcos said, "I do," as he stepped forward in anticipation.

She met his eyes, "Once you find your treasure, will you tell me everything?"

Marcos hesitated, scratched his ear, and then smiled and said, "Of course."

Jules pointed to the far end of the box canyon. She said, "Near the far wall is a cave; right at the base of the cliff, behind the rotted logs."

He pointed an accusing finger at her, "I knew you were hiding something!"

Jules shook her head. "You're the one that's hiding something."

Marcos tore at the debris that blocked the cave entrance. In a few minutes a way was cleared. He was covered with soot.

He held up a charred stump, and said, "Looks like there was a fire here once." He looked up and saw how the overhanging cliff would have sheltered it from the rain.

"It must have been a long time ago," he added.

As he moved one of the crumbling logs out of the way an ancient pistol was revealed.

He raised it reverently, and mused, "Perhaps my ancestor died defending this treasure."

Jules said, "More likely trying to steal it."

Marcos stared at her.

"What makes you think my ancestor was such a bad person?"

As they entered the cave, she asked, "What makes you think he was good? He carved up his chest, he scalped Indians, and he was ruthless."

Marcos nodded. "He was a man of power, in a brutal world. I think you can't fathom the sacrifices he made in the name of a greater good."

"No, that's not it," she replied, "I've never had much money, but I can't see how a treasure could drive you to do what he did to his body."

It was dark inside the cave. The sound of dripping water filled the silence. Marcos walked the perimeter quickly, and then stopped.

He said, "It seems like there's a tunnel here, but it has been filled in with sand. I'm going to get a shovel and a flashlight."

He paused at the entrance and warned Jules, "Don't go near the tunnel."

Jules replied, "Just relax, Marcos."

Robert DeMayo

Marcos exited and Jules took out a candle and lighter. She lit the candle and cautiously examined the cave. Water dripped down into clear pools, each drop echoing throughout the cave.

She saw a mound of sand in the middle and walked there, bending low so she didn't bang her head.

On the mound it was dry and she squatted, standing the candle in the sand.

She looked around, taking it all in.

Beyond the sound of the water dripping she heard the voice of Saan, on the reservation, saying, "She was scared, child, very scared. So she ran to the Cave Where The Water Always Drips and hid there."

Jules looked around with new eyes, her hands exploring the sand mound, feeling the soft impression on the top.

She remembered Saan also said, "When the water hit her, that's when she got pregnant."

Jules ran her hands under the sand, letting it sift through her fingers.

And then she heard Saan again, saying, "Your mother said she found that place once."

Jules said, "What really happened here, Saan?"

Then her hand encountered several objects; one was solid and heavy.

She extracted two ancient leather bundles from the sand mound. The smaller unrolled to reveal several containers of powder, and two manmade dolls. Jules lifted the dolls and examined them.

They were worn, and very old. One was male, the other female. The male doll had been broken.

She set them down, and was about to open the second bundle, which was heavier, when she heard Marcos approaching.

Quickly she reburied it.

When Marcos appeared she held up the two dolls.

"Look at these," said Jules. "They have to be hundreds of years old."

Marcos paused only long enough to confirm they were not made of gold.

He sniffed one of the containers of gray powder with disgust.

"Paint," he said.

Then he walked to the tunnel entrance and started shoveling.

After a few minutes the outline of a stone doorway became visible. Whoever had filled in the tunnel had only covered the entrance.

He proudly pointed at his discovery, "You see this? These are not natural stones — this was built." He shoveled faster, the exertion causing his body to flush with sweat. Several times he banged his elbows.

Jules examined the doorway, and then looked over the cave. "My Auntie talked about a place like this," she said.

Marcos had broken through to a clear tunnel. He frantically removed the dirt and stabbed the shovel into the sand.

He acknowledged Jules´s word, almost as an afterthought. "Really? What did she say about it?"

She replied, "She said it was a place where men weren't allowed."

Marcos almost fell down, outraged.

"Are you telling me you don't think I have a right to be here?" he shouted and grabbed the shovel. "You think maybe I should step outside?"

He stabbed at the sand again. His face turned a dark red. "That maybe it's sacred to someone whom I might offend?"

Jules realized she should have kept quiet. "I didn't say any of that."

He seemed disoriented, "Good, because it is pretty damn sacred to me."

He stopped suddenly and stared directly at Jules. Slowly he smiled.

"Now I see your plan," said Marcos. "You think if you can link this to your people that they can claim this as their treasure?"

She shook her head. "I told you, I'm not in this for the treasure."

Marcos grabbed her roughly. "Then tell me what you are really looking for, Jules."

He pushed her down, and when she moved to stand again he backhanded her with force.

A drop of blood flew off her face and landed in the sand.

The sky outside the entrance began to darken.

He loomed over her until she lay back submissively. There was a crazed look in his eyes that made her fear him for the first time. She raised her hands defensively as she talked, afraid of what he might do with the shovel.

"My father said that this cave never existed, that it was just a story," said Jules. "He was wrong."

Marcos laughed, "I still see no connection between this cave and your people. Do you think this is the only cave in Arizona with water in it?"

"What about the dolls and paint?" asked Jules.

"Trinkets left by a savage," said Marcos. Then he added, "What made you so certain the cave even existed?"

Jules paused, and then said, "My mother claimed that she found it years ago."

Her reply seemed to baffle Marcos.

He turned, walked over to the newly discovered tunnel, and asked sarcastically, "Do you really think your mother's people would have left this tunnel unexplored? That they wouldn't have discovered what lies beyond?"

Jules shook her head. "Maybe they didn't know about the tunnel, at least not in modern times," she said.

He disagreed, "That's not realistic. Someone would know."

She said, "Maybe the women knew, and they didn't let the men enter."

At this he started to laugh. "So that's why your mother never told anyone about it, right? And now you are carrying on the tradition."

He became serious again. "I'm tired of your stories. If you want to live you better stay put. If you follow me I will kill you."

He disappeared into the tunnel with the flashlight.

The candle was still lit, and by its light Jules lay on her back and stared at the ceiling. She had a bloody nose, and a fat lip.

As she wiped the blood off her face she looked up and saw a bloody handprint on the ceiling.

She stared at her red hand.

A drop of water let loose and hit her on the forehead.

Chapter Eleven

Fernando sat with his back to the wall. There was a log pinned against him, with a stake piercing his leg. He grinned at the pain, and said, "Puta!"

He wrenched the stake out, howling in pain, and then continued down the tunnel, now leaving a small blood trail.

Soon he emerged into a large cavern. The ceiling curved high above, blanketed with crystal-covered stalactites. They reflected the light of his torch, and illuminated the entire dome in a low glow.

The chamber in front of Fernando was still in shadows. He hollered, "Hello!" and then listened to his echo.

This was a big place.

He limped forward and found a large metal bowl blocking his way. He peered inside it, and saw a dark liquid filling the bowl.

It looked like blood.

Quickly he stepped away, repelled by a pungent smell, and afraid of what it could actually be.

Holding his torch forward he saw two horizontal tracks running out of each side of the bowl. The liquid flowed off into the darkness to his left and right.

Fernando touched his torch to the bowl and the liquid ignited — a burst of flame fire-balled up into the air with a deafening sound.

Fernando dropped to his knees and held both ears in pain; there was a trickle of blood coming out of one.

At the same time, flames shot out both sides of the bowl, and raced along the tracks into the darkness. Seconds later, fireballs burst into the air as the flames reached the next metal bowls hidden in the dark.

This went on like Chinese New Year for a solid minute, until the last explosion. Then all was silent while the smoke cleared.

Except for Fernando's cries of pain.

The first thing visible was the flaming metal bowls. They were actually made of gold.

They formed a large square with at least ten per side. The far side was not visible. Despite his pain, Fernando took notice.

Inside the square a huge object slowly emerged from the smoke. From its base it looked big, more like a small hill than a structure.

It was a pyramid; Aztec in design and stepped.

In the darkness its surface seemed to shimmer. Fernando fought through the fog that the pain had enveloped him in and stood. Everything was muted.

He yelled, "Hello," but could not hear his reply; his voice had been silenced.

As the smoke dissipated, the glow from the

flaming bowls reflected off the ceiling and flooded the entire cavern with light.

Fernando jumped when he saw a man standing at the base of the pyramid; the smoke had not completely cleared and swirled around his legs. He pulled out his pistol.

"Who are you?" demanded Fernando, loudly. He still could not hear his own question.

The man did not reply. He didn't move either.

He just stood there with his right arm pointing at his neck. He seemed to be grinning.

"You think your silence will frighten me?" challenged Fernando.

He raised his pistol and walked to the man.

He screamed, "You will answer my questions."

He raised his pistol and was about to fire when something about the man made him pause. Upon closer inspection he saw it was actually the desiccated remains of someone who died a painful death.

The man had been impaled on a stake to give the impression of standing. In his right hand he held a jewel-encrusted obsidian dagger that he had pushed through his own neck.

"A work of art," said Fernando.

He stared at the man's impaled body, and asked, "How long did you wait until you finally did it?" After a minute he added, "Do you have any living friends still here or did they all abandon you?"

He stepped around the body, and shouted, "Because I am not afraid of the dead!"

Fernando now saw that there was a main staircase leading to a temple on the top of the pyramid.

He paused on one of the bottom steps, and when he moved on there was a small puddle of blood from his leg wound. The blood slowly trickled into a drain on the side of the steps and disappeared into the pyramid.

He ascended, limping heavily.

He could see the top steps; they were actually covered with gold that had spilled over; lots of gold. There were masks, chains, coins, bars, all made of gold.

There seemed no end to the treasures!

Fernando sank to his knees in his moment of glory, and said, "It is mine!" Below him, the golden bowls glowed warmly, their reflection showing off the ceiling. Aside from his voice there was only silence.

He slowly climbed the staircase until he reached the gold. It was piled so thickly that the stairs were not visible.

He ran his hands through it; his eyes were wild with excitement.

Kamala appeared behind him, near the base of the staircase. She was now naked, her body covered with grey paint over which black spots and other designs had been neatly applied.

She pointed at the pyramid, and shouted, "Is this what you wanted? Do you need this to be happy?"

Fernando looked around, sensing something.

Then he saw her, but could not make out her muffled words.

She mouthed the words, "It is evil."

Fernando waved her off, and shouted back loudly, "Go back to the fire, woman; this treasure no longer concern you."

Kamala stood where she was, and watched. She had the look of a predator about her now, even though she didn't make a move to approach him.

She waited.

Fernando was half crazed as he attempted to reach the top level of the pyramid. He dug his boots into the gold like he was climbing through ice.

He giggled when some loose coins spilled on him, and shrieked, "Too much wealth to climb!"

The level area on the top of the pyramid was occupied by a square temple with framed doorways on three sides. The walls were covered with scenes of human sacrifice.

He climbed through the piles of gold and approached it reverently.

A golden throne marked the place of honor, facing west. Sitting in the chair was a dried out corpse that wore a flowing tunic. The man's skeleton was covered with chains of gold and precious stones.

Fernando walked to him, and said, "You're not Montezuma; I heard what happened to him."

He fingered the tunic, and examined the clothing the dead man was wearing. Inspecting one of the pieces of jewelry, he lifted it and slipped it in his pocket. He said, "You had good taste, I'll give you that much."

Kamala appeared behind him and slowly approached. She moved like a cougar.

Fernando was still engaged in conversation with the dead man, his deafness made him oblivious to her approach. He said to the skeleton, "You must be someone he trusted. He didn't want many people to know about this."

He broke off a finger to extract a ring and the whole hand crumbled under his touch.

Across the temple room was a pile.

Fernando moved closer and saw that it was actually a stack of bodies. What had once been about twenty men was now just a mass of bones and tattered flesh.

Fernando said, "Those must be your helpers."

Behind him, Kamala came into view. She looked fearsome as she walked right up behind him without drawing his attention.

She said, "You will end as they did."

Fernando turned in surprise; his hearing was returning.

He said, "This man deserves the treasure no more than you or I."

He pointed to the bodies, and said, "Look at what he did in the name of his king."

Kamala looked at the bodies but seemed unmoved. She said, "Leave this place, Fernando."

He tried again. "Kamala, we could share this. We could live like royalty."

She only replied, "This is an evil place."

Fernando approached the man on the throne, and shouted, "I am no more afraid of this man's evil magic than I was of the Indian witch they warned me of."

He grabbed the body by the chest, ripped the tunic apart, and said, "I can use this though."

Kamala screamed and attacked him. She was not the quiet girl from the box canyon, but had turned into a ferocious animal.

Fernando fought her off with fear in his eyes.

With difficulty, he finally shoved her to the ground. As she attempted to stand he threatened her with his pistol.

He shouted, "Obey me."

* * *

Marcos approached the pyramid and almost walked into what remained of the impaled guard. He jumped back in fright, and screamed, "Christ!"

The cavern was pitch black, except for the small area lit by his flashlight. He stared at the impaled man in horror.

The stale stench of death in the air seemed to have a source far greater than one dead man. Marcos could sense it, and it made him shiver.

Suddenly he turned, as if to flee, and it was only with great difficulty that he could convince himself to go on. He felt like he was in a crypt.

He bent forward to control his breathing, and stayed that way for a few minutes before continuing.

As Marcos passed the impaled guardian he roughly snatched the dagger out of the dead man´s hand; the fingers crumbled away.

At the base of the pyramid he paused again; his flashlight only illuminating the bottom portion of the staircase. His light was dimming slightly and it worried him.

As he ascended his footsteps echoed.

He heard the echo and got the creepy feeling that he was not alone.

He stopped and shouted, "Who's there?" But there was no answer.

When he neared the top of the pyramid he began to see a golden glow. And then the treasure came into view. He hurried to the top, fell to his knees and ran his hands through the gold.

Breathing deeply, with tears in his eyes, he said, "I claim this treasure in the name of the DeNiza family."

He took off his backpack and set it down, and added, "I claim it for Fernando and Antonio."

Then he ran from one piece to the next and with each one he touched, his face seemed to glow more.

He examined a golden object with precious stones inlaid. His eyes were glossy, as he said, "Mine."

Setting down his backpack, he started filling it with whatever gold objects he could reach. He filled it, but was then forced to empty out some because the pack now weighed too much to lift.

Then he painfully raised it onto his shoulders.

His flashlight dimmed again, and he took one last look at the treasure all around him, smiled, and promised, "I will be back, don't worry."

Back in the cave with the dripping water Jules opened the second leather-wrapped bundle.

Inside she found a White Stone, encircled by a band of gold. Strangely, right next to it was a plastic bag with a letter inside.

When she examined the letter, she was surprised to see her name on the envelope. She opened it.

> *Dear Jules,*
>
> *After your visit several years ago, I learned the truth behind the Cave we talked about from a dying elder. Since that day I feared you would try to find it, and being your mother's daughter, I thought you probably would.*
>
> *I have no doubt that the stories I told you are true, but this cave has a darker side as well. The elder told me that there is a tunnel that leads from the cave, and it goes to an evil place. In the olden days only women were allowed to come here, and their duty was to keep the men away. Men who entered the next chamber lost themselves and could not be trusted.*
>
> *Our legends stated that for a man to even breathe the air of the box canyon would be their end. This may have been an exaggeration, but it kept the men away. If you have come here with a man who has passed through that tunnel then get away.*
>
> *I pray this letter finds you safe, Saan.*

Jules folded the letter and put it in her pocket. She then reached for the White Stone to examine it. The moment her bloodied hand touched it, the stone began to glow. It seemed to pulse as its low glow lit up the chamber.

Although common sense told her to get away, she found herself walking toward the tunnel. When only a few feet away, the wind quickly extinguished her candle, leaving her with only the pulsing light of the White Stone to show her way.

Cautiously she entered the low tunnel and crept through it. After a while she felt herself approaching an opening where it exited into a large cavern.

Jules crouched there listening. In the distance she could hear Marcos raving. His tone alone made her realize Saan was right.

When she saw his flashlight coming her way, she backed into the tunnel again, and made her way to what she now regarded as the Cave Where The Water Always Dripped.

She continued down the tunnel and eventually passed an old spike trap. This was where Marcos´ forebear had met his fate. Even though the mechanism was ancient, the dry conditions of the cave had preserved the wood. Jules moved the log back and reset the trap.

She paused and listened.

She could hear Marcos approaching. Forced to crawl, his treasure was spilling onto the back of his head and he cursed repeatedly.

Jules made it to the Cave Where the Water Always Drips and listened again.

She heard a whipping sound, and then a "thud."

Marcos emitted a piercing scream. Then, all was silent.

In the Cave Where The Water Always Drips Jules stopped at the dry sand mound and waited. There was no sound at all coming from the tunnel, only the dripping of water all around her.

After a few minutes she exhaled.

She took out the White Stone and looked at it, and said, "I don't think you were ever meant to leave this cave," and buried it in the sand.

Then she picked up the two dolls and placed them on top of the sand pile. "Maybe someone wanted you to end up together."

Next she reached into her pocket and took out the photograph of her mother and Saan.

After staring at it for a minute, she placed it with the dolls, and said, "I think you both would have liked this."

She looked around, and added, "To be here."

She relaxed, and wiped the blood and sweat from her face. Looking up, she stared at the bloody handprint again.

As she did she became angry, faced the tunnel and shouted, "Treasures that drive weak men insane? Isn't that what you said, Marcos?"

She looked over the cave, and then outside.

She shouted again, "Got nothing to say? Is that really what Fernando died for—for a treasure?"

She squinted her eyes and listened.

In a weak voice, she said, "Where there is lightness, there is darkness."

Jules closed her eyes and sat motionlessly. Her expressions drained from her face, and her breathing slowed.

She sat like this for a while, with her eyes shut; when she opened them she was alert and focused.

From her side she took the container of gray powder and opened it. She let some water drip into it and started to mix the paint.

In the tunnel Marcos grunted and cursed, and then painfully emerged. He was red with rage, and held his arm which was bleeding. He was also covered with sweat and dirt.

In his hand was the obsidian dagger.

Marcos approached Jules from behind; he was breathing heavily, but somehow she appeared not to have heard him coming.

He said, "You had your chance to leave. I warned you."

Marcos walked over to the mound and picked up one of the dolls—the male doll.

He said, "You want me to believe you are more interested in this?" He ripped the Male doll into two pieces and tossed them into a pool of water.

He shouted, "To hell with your Gods."

There was a faint echo in the cave of Fernando shouting the same words.

Marcos stood, one foot on the mound, a hand on his hip. "The world will not believe what I have seen. What I have rediscovered!"

He reached forward, grabbed Jules by the shoulder and spun her around. Just as he was about to scream something at her he saw her face.

He stepped back in shock.

Jules had covered her face with grey paint, but that was the smallest part of her transformation. Her eyes had become those of an aggressive animal; one summing up its prey. They did not look like they belonged to Jules, but their stare was piercing Marcos.

Marcos staggered backward, unable to believe what he was staring at. What she had become.

He pointed at her with the dagger.

"What are you really searching for, Jules?" he asked, while she kept staring at him from under her brows. "You think you can learn something from what happened here?"

He took a quick step and lunged at her. She stood her ground, her gaze unflinching, unafraid. Her strange composure made him falter, and he didn't follow through with his attack.

Instead, he asked, "Is it somehow going to bring you closer to your so called People? Or your mother?"

She glared at him quietly, but he continued taunting, "The truth is, you are here all alone. There's nobody to help you."

Robert DeMayo

Jules´ demeanor brightened suddenly; she covered her mouth to hide an almost girlish giggle. Her expressions now seemed more like Kamala's.

Marcos kept raving, until he saw the serious look return to her face.

She said confidently, "I am not alone."

Marcos stared at her in confusion.

"What?"

She continued, "There is somebody, somebody hears me, and somebody watches over me. I am not alone."

Marcos cried, "You've lost your mind."

Jules ignored him and moved to the cave exit into the box canyon. As she got close the wind caught her hair and blew it everywhere.

Marcos called after her, "You messed with my treasure! I can't let you leave to tell the world about it!"

Jules stepped out into the box canyon, unconcerned with the pursuit of a man with a dagger.

Without even turning, she said, "You should never have gone inside."

Chapter Twelve

Fernando sat on the throne, his eyes were crazy. While rubbing the golden handrail of the throne he spoke of his plans.

By his feet knelt Kamala, staring at the ground submissively.

"With this wealth I will start an empire," Fernando said.

He admired the workmanship on another piece of gold while he talked. He breathed on it, and rubbed it to a shine.

"I will have power," he said to his reflection in the gold, "and my name will echo through history."

Off to the side was the body of the man who originally had sat on the throne. Fernando looked at it. He got up, walked to it, and crushed the skull under his feet.

"Your time here is over. It is now mine."

He lifted what was left of the skeleton and tossed it on top of the pile of dried out bodies. He was almost giddy. "Out with the old!" he exclaimed.

Then, for a long time, he stared at the pile of human remains.

He looked at the body he'd just added to the eerie heap, and said, "You were a smart one. If one of these men had escaped, this treasure would be gone now. There'd be nothing left but an empty pyramid."

He turned and stared at Kamala. Her face remained passive, but she had well caught the madness in his eyes.

Fernando mumbled, "It really would be stupid for me to not follow your example."

Kamala stood and stepped backward, and as she did she unconsciously placed a hand over her belly. Fernando took a step toward her and extended one arm, as if to embrace her.

He smiled and acted calm, but he was not fooling her. Kamala had already seen the club-like gold object he held in the other hand behind his back.

She stated coldly, "This treasure has poisoned your spirit."

Fernando smiled, "Come with me, we will..."

He swung, and just before he struck Kamala's arm shot forward and she plunged her knife into his shoulder. His blow collapsed and he howled in pain as Kamala disappeared into the darkness.

Later, Fernando exited the tunnel that led into the Cave Where The Water Always Drips. He was dragging a tarp filled with gold, and moved slowly.

He saw Kamala sitting on the sand mound. Despite the gray paint on her face she again looked like the young woman who saved him and sheltered him all those days.

She held her belly, which showed the beginning stages of pregnancy. He wondered if this was why she had been sick.

She said, "You remember what happened here? What you did?"

This stopped Fernando in his tracks. He answered, "Yes. I remember."

Kamala rubbed her tummy again, and Fernando stared at it, suddenly aware of the possible consequence to his actions.

Kamala indicated her abdomen, and stated, "This is not your treasure." He looked at her in confusion, and asked, "What do you mean?"

Kamala said again, "This is not your treasure, and it will bring you no happiness."

He seemed to grasp that she believed she was pregnant. He asked, "You are with child?"

She said flatly, "Not your child."

Fernando flew into a rage.

He shouted, "Then whose?"

Kamala smiled as she remembered her embrace with Aditsan by the river. He had flicked water in her face and for a moment she had forgotten where she was. She could see his eyes clearly.

She said to Fernando, "You leave a treasure far greater than the one you steal."

He screamed, "Do not mock me!"

Kamala pointed to the tunnel, and said, "I did not tell you about the other cave because I knew it would be the end of you."

"You kept it from me!" he said angrily.

Fernando took out his pistol and checked it over. He said, "Why would you do that if you didn't want it for yourself?"

She shook her head. "I have no use for it, it destroys men. For a while I thought you might stay and be nice. I should have known that you would not give up until you found it."

Slowly, she backed out the cave entrance, into the box canyon still crackling with the burning trees by the entrance. The flames were thrown everywhere by violent gusts of wind.

Above, the clouds were dark and menacing; lightning flashed.

Fernando limped forward, a tarp of gold in tow. He approached Kamala and said, "I am sorry it has to end this way."

He raised his pistol.

A flash of resignation crossed Kamala's face. "You are determined."

From ten feet away Fernando pointed the gun at her heart, and said, "I am."

Kamala smiled at him. "People who have faith and understand do not need weapons."

He screamed, "Damn you!"

Just as he pulled the trigger a bolt of lightning hit his gun and sent him flying. The bullet ricocheted off a far wall in the canyon. Fernando's hand was red and shaking.

Kamala and Fernando stumbled away from the cave entrance as one of the flaming trees collapsed on itself; engulfing the gun. A shower of sparks rose high in the air.

Kamala spoke. "At first, I brought you here so you wouldn't kill the other Indian. I liked the listener, Aditsan. He did not deserve to die that day."

Fernando was scared now. He stared at her, and then looked at his blistered hand in disbelief.

"Witch," he whispered.

She replied sadly. "I always felt you might die here. It is what happens to men who find the treasure — they lose themselves. But I thought I could keep it from you."

Kamala lowered her head and began to cry, and the rain became torrential. A rapid stream flowed through the box canyon into the exit tunnel; from all around the water funneled into the box canyon.

Fernando dragged his bundle along the rapid little stream, while Kamala walked on the other side, watching him.

He stared back at her every so often, but seemed unable to talk. He continued to the exit from the Box Canyon.

Her eyes were full of pain and sadness.

She said, "Fernando, please."

He took a step into the exit chute, then paused and pulled his bundle next to him. The water hit it and pushed him forward.

For a minute the storm seemed to abate and Fernando looked at Kamala, who was standing a few feet away.

He said, "I'm sorry."

She looked vulnerable as she extended her hand. He looked at it, and reached to touch her, but the gold was pushed forward again by the current and dragged Fernando with it.

He stopped himself, but couldn't hold it for long.

Fernando hesitated and moved toward her; his expression changed, as if he grasped that he was leaving something sacred.

She looked him in the eye. "Stay."

She began to sob, when suddenly the raven flew in and landed on her shoulder. It stared at Fernando, and cawed.

At the same time Aditsan emerged from the other side of the exit tunnel and seized Fernando by the wrists. He was holding his breath as he grabbed the Spaniard, and Fernando stared at him in disbelief.

At once Fernando lost his footing and he and his bag of gold were flushed through the shoot, which had suddenly become a river.

Aditsan was taken with him, leaving Kamala standing alone.

* * *

It was raining hard, and the sky was dark. Jules walked backward toward the campsite.

Marcos pursued her, slowed down by his pack. He still had the dagger in his hand.

In a strange voice, he said, "Let's just get this over with." But as he stepped to assault her, the look in her eyes made him freeze.

There was still something different about her, an eerie change that scared him deeply.

Lighting crashed into the far wall of the box canyon and Marcos jumped and screamed. Jules didn't flinch.

She still seemed to be focused somewhere else, as she said, "You don't have to do this."

The rain was coming down so hard they could barely see. Marcos looked at the exit out of the box canyon, which was now half filled with whirling water. It looked dangerous.

He hesitated.

"I'm sorry," he said. "But I can't leave you here to steal the treasure."

He raised his dagger again and walked toward her.

As he approached, his eyes narrowed. "You think this was a place of safety? You think someone had a nice happy home here?"

Jules circled, so the exit chute was behind him.

He continued, "This place is a deathtrap—look around."

She did, and saw that from all around the rain funneled down into the drain.

"If there's death here, it's because of you," she said. "What I sought was creation, or love, or life — something that would make it all make sense.

Marcos smiled, and grabbed the knife tightly. "If you weren't so obsessed with these fairy tales you may have been part of my discovery."

She reminded him, "I never cared about it."

He stared at her, and said, "You're just a scared little girl."

Jules stood tall, and summoned the last of her energy.

She said calmly, "I may have been once."

As he raised his arm to strike with the knife she took one quick step and kicked Marcos in the chest.

"Not anymore," she added as she swiftly set her foot back on the ground.

The kick and the weight of his pack sent him backwards into the water-filled tunnel where he cannon-balled upon impact.

For a moment he was visible, his body and the backpack blocking the flow of water. Then the force of it took hold of the whole bundle and flushed everything through.

Jules was left standing in the Box Canyon alone, looking at the tunnel, which was now almost a river.

She looked up and the rain began to wash away the gray powder that covered her face.

The Cave Where The Water Always Drips

Marcos was flung down the scree. His backpack was torn to shreds, the gold scattered in the raging waters all around him.

He clawed at the gold washing away, and howled, "No! My treasure!"

He had rolled out of the stream and managed to pick up a few odd pieces. He stuck them in his shirt, but cried out in frustration as he watched the rest disappear. "I cannot leave without proof!"

With determined force, he stood and tried to regain his composure. He controlled his breathing and assessed his situation.

Then a sound behind him made him look around. From nowhere a raven suddenly appeared flying directly at him. It hit him in the forehead with its claws extended.

Marcos stood there, stunned. Blood was running into his eyes.

He became suddenly aware that water was filling the narrow canyon. He realized if he didn't get out of there he would die.

A look of panic crossed his face.

In the back of his head he heard old Saan´s voice warning, "Do something wrong and the rains come."

Marcos turned and started to run down the canyon.

The rain had just ended and everything was still dripping. Jules walked down the narrow canyon, staying to the side where the stream was only a few inches deep.

The washes she passed were all still running, but the flow seemed to be slowing down. What did flow was filled with soap suds from the roots of the Yucca plants that got caught in the water.

She searched for Marcos as she walked, calling, "Marcos!"

As she approached a turn in the canyon she saw a large pile of logs and branches. Near the bottom a flash of color caught her attention.

She moved quickly to the log pile and found Marcos pinned under the debris.

There was a truckload of logs on top of him and it was a miracle that he was still alive, even if just barely. His head was just above the water that had piled up the logs and was still rushing under it.

Jules hurried to him.

He tried to smile, and said, "Now this is how you imagined I would end up, isn't it?"

She denied it, "It isn't at all. I never wanted anything bad to happen to you."

He moaned and said in a strained voice, "No, I suppose you are telling the truth."

She tried to move a few logs but Marcos howled in pain. "Stop!" It was hopeless.

A roaring sound upstream got their attention. Another rainstorm upstream had caused a surge of water; it was now coming crashing down the canyon.

It hit the bend and all but covered Marcos.

Jules frantically tried to lift him out. He screamed and coughed through the water. "It's no good. I'm dead anyway . . . you wouldn't believe the wall of water that hit me."

"I cannot let it end like this," said Jules.

"Leave," said Marcos. "Save yourself."

He stared at her for a moment, and then said, "I have this coming to me."

Jules stood her ground. The water was rising. She asked, "Tell me what Fernando told Antonio right before he died."

Marcos hesitated, and then said, "It was nothing, really. He said only one word."

Jules pleaded, "Tell me!"

Even now Marcos paused. He was having trouble breathing and struggled to raise his head a bit higher.

Jules held her breath in anticipation.

* * *

Antonio was leading his mule down the large canyon. A sudden storm had just ended, and the sun was out.

He reached the fork and saw Fernando on the ground. He was battered beyond belief.

Antonio ran to him, and gasped, "Brother, what has become of you?"

Fernando waved away the question, and said, weakly, "There is no time, open my shirt."

Antonio did and was horrified at what he saw. He asked, "Fernando, who did this?"

Robert DeMayo

Fernando almost smiled at the question, and then painfully pulled a piece of soft leather from his belt. When he opened it a gold coin fells to the ground.

Fernando looked at the symbol on the top of the piece of leather, and then placed the leather over his chest and painfully padded it down.

He said to Fernando, "You must go back for me Antonio, I was a fool. Use the map."

Antonio pleaded, "Tell me what you found."

Before he could reply the canyon was filled with the faint sound of singing. A gust of wind blew through, and then it was gone.

Fernando screamed, and pulled his brother to him.

With wild eyes he yelled at Antonio, "Kamala!"

Jules had a flash of old Saan speaking the same name all those years ago.

In Fernando's eye passed the moments he had shared in the canyon with Kamala. He forgot her sickness or the untrusting look in her eyes, all he saw was the positive.

While Antonio anxiously sat by his side, Fernando stared off into the distance and remembered: her first appearance coming out of the log while Fernando was hiding, smiling with a flower in her hair, her reaction to the adobe hut he had built, preparing him a bowl of soup while he was injured, holding up a string of trout; and then finally Kamala crying, and obviously pregnant.

The memories became overwhelming as he revisited Kamala's sad face and her timid question, "Do you love me?" He screamed.

Chapter Thirteen

Jules was blown away by what Marcos told her.

"He made the map to get back to her!" she exclaimed.

Another surge of water headed toward Marcos.

He blurted out, "You think a woman was more important to him than that treasure?"

Jules replied, "He said 'Kamala'."

Marcos nodded weakly.

Jules was quiet.

He finally asked, "You will still tell the world of my discovery?"

She shook her head, and said, "Nobody's ever going to know, Marcos. It was never meant to be found."

Eyes filled with disbelief Marcos frantically tried to free himself.

"What are you saying?" he asked, panting heavily.

Jules stepped back.

She said, "When I was young I heard about the cave and the hidden canyon and was told they never existed."

Marcos struggled to breathe.

Jules said, "I don't care about the treasure. I never did. I just had to see for myself if the cave was real."

He was now exhausted from his efforts to stay alive. He coarsely asked, "Will you stop with these fantasies? The world must know of my discovery."

She shook her head again. "It's over, Marcos," said Jules. "I returned what I could find and hid the entrance."

He howled and tried to wrench free but it was no good. Another surge of water came through and forced him to squeeze his eyes shut and hold his breath.

One last time he lifted his head out of the flood and looked at her.

He said quickly, "I was a fool."

Then the water engulfed him and he was gone.

Jules climbed a steep scree and scrambled to safety.

Antonio cradled his brother's head while looking around fearfully. He pleaded, "Wake up brother, I don't like it here."

Fernando stirred, and opened his eyes.

"I was a fool," he said weakly.

Suddenly an arrow came whizzing down from above and sank into Fernando's chest. Antonio jumped backwards, dropping the coin in the process.

He screamed, "No!"

A quick glance at Fernando confirmed the arrow had finished him off. This was too much for Antonio He started ripping off his breastplate and armor. He flung his helmet to the ground.

Tearing open his shirt he shouted at the cliff tops.

Over and over he yelled, "Shoot me! Shoot me!"

High above Grey Wolf watched Antonio for a minute, then shook his head and backed away. He moved to his small fire where he set down his bow and sat.

Across from him sat Aditsan who was thoroughly drenched.

Grey Wolf said, "I would have let you kill him."

Aditsan was deep in thought and seemed unconcerned.

He shrugged.

Finally, Aditsan said, "I never cared what would happen to either of them."

Antonio's screams could still be heard echoing up from below.

Grey Wolf said with a sigh, "Take the other before he drives us crazy."

Aditsan shook his head again, and said, "I am focused on other things."

Grey Wolf smiled, and lifted his pipe. After a moment he began to chant.

Below Antonio grabbed the lead to his mule and walk away. He was still screaming.

Spring, everything was blooming.

Kamala, very pregnant, munched on a piece of trout with relish.

The raven landed next to her.

She said, "I had to leave. It's worth leaving for fish."

The raven cawed.

"I told you I wouldn't be long," said Kamala. She tossed a piece of fish to the raven and he hopped forward to retrieve it.

Then she held up a leather bag with a feathered design, and she said excitedly, "And, I have a new gift from Aditsan."

The raven hopped over to inspect it.

By her side was the Spanish helmet. It was set on a rock, as if attending the meal.

"He liked fish," said Kamala, "you remember."

The raven flew over to the helmet, hopped on top, and defecated, and then cawed loudly.

Kamala laughed and began to sing.

Not far away Grey Wolf sat by his fire. Aditsan approached and handed him a fur.

On the cliff tops the winds were sharp and he gratefully wrapped himself.

Once comfortable he set out to light his pipe.

From a distance he heard a woman singing, and he paused. The melody echoed throughout the canyon.

Grey Wolf sat up and listened. The singing went on for a moment, and then stopped.

Aditsan looked in the direction of the singing and smiled. He seemed to relax.

Grey Wolf smiled as well, and relit his pipe.

THE END.

Robert DeMayo

About the author

Robert DeMayo took up traveling at the age of twenty when he left his job as a bio-medical Engineer to explore the world. Over the next 20 years he traveled to every corner of the globe—with a preference for overland journeys—and experienced close to 100 countries.

Subsequent trips were funded by journalism, importing, and odd work along the way. A few of the jobs he picked up were: bartending in London, swinging a sledge hammer in Israel (for $8 a day), rewiring an intercom at a brothel in Australia, and teaching English in Bangkok.

During his travels he worked extensively for the travel section of *The Telegraph*, out of Hudson, N.H. His first assignment was to drive from New Hampshire to Panama in 1988, writing feature articles on the way. He is a member of *The Explorers Club* and *The Archaeological Institute of America.*

For three years he worked as Marketing Manager for a company called *Eos* that served as the travel office for six non-profit organizations. Tours marketed included dives to the *Titanic* and the *Bismarck*, Antarctic voyages, and African safaris, as well as archaeological tours throughout the world.

After 9/11 he worked for three years as a driver/guide in Alaska (horseback and hiking in the Yukon, and historical tours of Skagway and The White Pass), and as a 4x4 jeep guide in Arizona. He is currently the General Manager for a jeep tour company called *A Day in the West* based out of Sedona, Arizona.

He now resides full time in Sedona, AZ with his wife, Diana, and two girls, Tavish (10) and Saydrin (8).

Robert DeMayo